Intruders
The Continuing Adventures of a Young Cowboy

Stu Campbell

ISBN: 978-0-9962019-0-2

6   5   4   3   2   1

Edited by Mira Perrizo
Cover and text design by D.K. Luraas
Cover painting by Larry Jones, Bouse, Arizona
Author photo by Elizabeth Dobbs

Printed in the United States of America

Contents

Tough Times

Things weren't good at the Wilson Ranch going into the winter. Bud had been to town and had an appointment at the doctor's office after the trial of the drunken hunter, and the news wasn't good.

I walked up to Bud and Sally while they were talking and overheard their conversation.

"Just what did the doc have to say?" Sally was concerned.

"It wasn't too good," replied Bud. "He did a lot of tests and won't really know until he gets the results. But he told me he suspected leukemia. Or, it could be multiple sclerosis."

"What's that?"

"It's a form of cancer," continued Bud, "but he's not sure, yet. He'll call in a couple of days when he finds out."

"What will it do?" Now Sally was very concerned. She hadn't seen her father in ill health at any time during her life, other than when his horse fell on him and he'd broken his foot a few years ago.

"I don't know anything about it," said Bud. "But there's no sense in worrying about it yet. We've got a ranch to run. Right now, we've only got the daily chores to do, but soon we'll be adding to that. So, for right now, let's do our chores and get ready for spring. We don't have any colts to halter break this winter, we sold all the weaners last fall at our horse sale. We don't have any coming two-year-old colts for you to start riding this spring, Honey, since we sold all of the yearlings last fall. It will be a fairly easy winter this year. Honey, you and Pat will be plenty busy with the first calf heifers during February, and the older cows should start calving around the first of March.

"I think we've got a wedding to do in May, and then the dudes start arriving before Memorial Day. So we'll be busy until then."

"You'll let me know what the doctor says?" Sally was still very concerned, although Bud had tried to shift the conversation from him to the ranch.

"Yes, daughter, I'll let you know."

"Good or bad?"

"Certainly. But don't count on it being all bad. Remember, things always work out the way they're supposed to."

Thanksgiving came and we all enjoyed a big supper. My mother called and after a few minutes of talking to her, she asked to talk to Sally. I didn't overhear their conversation; I left the room.

"What did my mother say to you?"

"Not much," answered Sally. "We talked mostly about the wedding. They're coming, you know. She sounded surprised when I told her I was helping you do the feeding."

"I figured that," I said. "Is that all?"

"She did say to keep an eye on you and I am supposed to tell you to be a good boy," she answered, laughing.

"That sounds like my mom," I said.

A few days after Thanksgiving, Bud got a call from the doctor. Sally asked, "What's the verdict?"

"He doesn't know," answered Bud. "I'll have to go to town and have some more tests done. The doc doesn't want to go out on a limb and make any guesses. I suppose that's all right. I don't want him guessing either."

Two days later, Bud went to the doctor. He returned and informed everyone that he didn't know anything more than before he went. "The doc will call with the results of the tests when he gets them." He sounded very positive when he said that, but had a hard time concealing the look of concern on his face.

The winter came with a fury. There was a lot of snow and it was very cold. We became concerned about the broodmare band, so one morning Pat and I saddled a couple of horses, loaded them in the two-ton truck, and went to look for them. We drove for about three hours then unloaded the horses by backing up to a rise in the ground, and started to look for our broodmare bunch.

"It's sure a lot nicer in the truck than in the saddle today," Pat said, as we rode away.

"Yep," I answered. "I suppose that truck will look pretty nice when we return."

It was cold and we rode in silence. The wind was blowing in another storm and I hoped we could find the horses before the storm hit.

We'd rode for about an hour before I spotted some tracks in the snow.

"There's tracks over here," I yelled at Pat.

He rode over and looked at the tracks. "They're headed the wrong way," he said. "They've been drifting with the storms an' they're gettin' a long ways from their home range. We ought to see if we can get around 'em an' push 'em closer to home. If we can do that, we might have to start bringin' some hay out for them, just to keep 'em closer to home."

We started out at a trot, following the tracks. Soon we found the broodmares and started pushing them toward where we had left the truck. I felt better about pushing the bunch toward the truck, as the wind was now at our back and it didn't feel as cold as it was.

We saw the truck in the distance and the broodmares were headed toward it. By the time we reached the truck the mares had gathered around it and were waiting for us.

We loaded our horses in the truck and got into the cab.

"Turn the heater on full blast," I said.

"It'll be cold air," said Pat.

"It can't be no colder than the air I been in the last couple of hours," I said. "If there's any warmth to it at all, it'll be better than what I've been feelin'."

Pat laughed and turned on the heater. "The horses will probably follow us all the way to the gate, thinkin' they'll get fed. We better bring some hay out tonight to get started. It'll help keep 'em around here. We're goin' to have to come out here an' feed them every day once we get started. It'll be you an' me. I don't think Bud will be able to help us much."

"I think we can handle it," I said. "Did you get a count on them? I didn't, there was too much millin' around to get a good count. Have you heard anything about Bud's condition?"

"I didn't get a good count, but I didn't notice anybody missin'. I think Bud's condition is a little worse than he wants to let on, but don't say that I said that."

We drove to the gate. I opened it and Pat drove through. After I'd closed the gate, I went to get in the passenger side of the truck and Pat was sitting in my spot.

"You drive," he said, "I'm tired of chauffeurin' you an' them horses around!"

Laughing, I got in the driver's side and started toward the ranch.

At supper, Pat informed Bud that we'd needed to start feeding the broodmares.

"We'll start in the morning. I've been toying with the idea Honey's dad had about feeding the cattle in the afternoon so they'd all calve in the mornings. If we take care of the horses in the morning, we can take care of the cattle in the afternoons. We should probably start feeding the saddle horses, too. We can throw them some hay on the way to feed the broodmares."

Our routine was changed, but the chores got done. All the animals on the ranch were fed regularly.

Christmas was approaching and Bud suggested that I go to town to do some Christmas shopping.

"There's too much to do around here for me to leave," I said.

"Nonsense! Don't you think I can do anything? I'll help Pat feed in the mornings and afternoons and we'll get everything done. Even the cook can help if needed—he's done it in the past. You go to town and take Sally with you. You can both do your shopping. And don't forget to get me something! The next day, Pat can go to town, then the cook, and then I'll take Missus Abercrombie and we'll do our shopping. That's the plan! Tomorrow, while we're feeding the horses, we'll get a Christmas tree."

The next day, Sally and I went to town in my truck. I had no idea what I was going to buy for anyone, let alone Missus Abercrombie. Sally gave me some ideas on the way to town and we decided that she could make the selections and I'd pay for them. Of course, I'd select something for me to give to Sally, although I had no idea what.

I left Sally at the department store and went to the saddle shop. I finally decided to get Sally a new pair of shotgun chaps. The chink chaps she had were still good, but chink chaps are a summer chap. The shotgun chaps would provide more warmth during the winter. I put the new chaps in the back of the truck and went back to the department store to get Sally.

Sally had made her purchases and mine. While she was waiting for me, she had all of the items gift wrapped and tagged. I did pick up some gifts for my mother and dad and Tommy and Betty and mailed them to our ranch. Christmas had never been so easy. When we got to the ranch, I took Sally's chaps to the bunkhouse, borrowed some wrapping paper from Missus Abercrombie, wrapped the chaps and put them under the tree that Missus Abercrombie had decorated.

The next day, Pat went to town and Bud, Sally, and I did the feeding chores. I watched Bud closely as we fed, he was slowing down, and I wondered just what was wrong. But he did insist on doing his part, even though Sally and I both objected strongly.

"I'll do this," he said, as I tried to take a pitchfork from him to shovel the hay off. "What do you think I am, an old man?"

I didn't say anything, but Sally said, "Yes. Just how old are you?"

"Never mind. I'll do this from this side and you do it from that side. Drive Honey!"

Then the cook went to town and finally, Bud and Missus Abercrombie went.

With all the Christmas shopping done, we settled back into the regular ranch routine. It took a lot of time to do the chores and the daylight was getting shorter each day.

On Christmas Eve, Bud said, "We'll do the morning chores then open presents around noon tomorrow, unless you want to get up an hour earlier in the morning."

Everyone agreed to opening presents around noon. We were all tired and the cold weather was taking its toll on everyone.

I was surprised when I opened my present from Sally. It was a pair of shotgun chaps. I almost blurted out, "Great minds think along the same lines," but managed to keep quiet. I didn't want to spoil the surprise I had for her.

"How did you know the right size?" The chaps fit perfectly. "When did you get 'em? You didn't go to the saddle shop."

"I got your size off your pants. Then I asked Daddy to pick them up when he went to town. It was simple."

When she opened her present, she was surprised. "Great minds think along the same lines!"

I was glad I hadn't said that.

"How did you get my size?"

"The same way you got mine," I answered. "Only I had to get them myself."

"You mean you've been looking at my butt?" Sally was teasing me now and laughing as she made the last comment.

Bud shot me a disapproving look, but smiled quickly.

"Only when necessary," I answered. "Only when necessary!"

The rest of the presents were being opened and I was very curious. Sally hadn't told me what she had gotten for me to give everyone.

When the presents were opened, and the recipients remarked, "That's just what I needed! How did you know?" I simply pointed to Sally and said, "I had a lot of help."

I opened a present from Missus Abercrombie that really surprised me. It was an electric heater.

"How am I goin' to use this?"

"You'll find a way," replied Missus Abercrombie. "At least Bud said you will." I accepted the gift, thanked Missus Abercrombie, but had no idea how I'd use it.

Bud gave Sally a new saddle, complete with her initials on the stirrup fenders and horn. She was certainly surprised and very pleased.

"The initials aren't right," she said. "Did you forget I'm changing my name when I get married?"

"No, daughter, I didn't forget. But I didn't think you wanted me to have them put 'Missus Honey' on it. We'll make it right when the time comes. Now quit this talk, can't you see you're making Honey blush?"

I felt selfconscious at the mention of Missus Honey, and started to feel flushed.

Christmas afternoon was spent doing the afternoon chores. A little reflection around the tree and we all retired for the evening.

On a ranch, there aren't any real holidays when there is livestock to be taken care of.

New Years Eve was spent about the same way, other than Pat firing a shotgun into the air at midnight. Bud made some comment about everyone having a prosperous new year and we all retired for the night.

The new year started out the same as every other day. The feeding chores took up most of the day, but there was some free time. Occasionally, Sally and I would walk up a hill and go for a sleigh ride. Trying as hard as she could, Sally couldn't convince her dad, Missus Abercrombie, Pat, or the cook to go with us. We tried to go at least once a week during January, and it was only when we'd gotten all the chores done and it wasn't too cold.

Toward the end of January, I was at the new calving pens. I'd driven the truck to the pens to do the feeding, when I noticed one of the heifers trying to calve. She looked like she was having some trouble, one foot of the calf was already out, and so I decided to give her a hand, even though I didn't have a horse handy.

I was having a hard time getting the heifer out of the corral on foot when Sally showed up, riding one of the coming three-year-old colts. It was real difficult to run through the snow on foot.

"What's the matter, cowboy, having a hard time?"

"Yep," I said, catching my breath. It had been difficult trying to run in the snow to head the heifer. "If you lend me your horse, I'll get her out an' into one of the pens under the shed so I can help her. Better hurry though, if she keeps runnin' around, she'll go ahead an' calve without the benefit of my assistance."

"Well, cowboy, just step back out of the way and I'll get that heifer out for you. She's not too much for me."

Sally entered the corral and got the heifer into the alley. I went ahead and opened a gate into a pen under the shed. By the time Sally got the heifer into the small pen, both feet of the calf were out.

"It looks like she's goin' to have this calf all by herself," I said, as I closed the gate. "Let's give her some time an' see if she'll do it by herself."

We went inside a small room we'd enclosed under the shed. We planned on using it for storing some medicines, vaccines, and the like. We had electricity and a refrigerator in the room. I'd put the electric heater Missus Abercrombie had given me in there and I sure appreciated it. After about fifteen minutes we went to check on the heifer.

She was up and licking a black and white calf whose head was bobbing up and down. The calf was still wet and the heifer was cleaning him off. The calf was making some feeble attempts to stand.

"I think things are all right here," I said. "Let's go to the house."

"No," said Sally. "I want to watch. Theses newborn calves are so cute! It's amazing how they struggle to get up the first time, fall, and try again. And their mothers can't even help them. They all have determination. And they seem to know right where to go to get fed. That has to be instinct; nobody has been around to teach them."

"It's get up an' eat or die for them," I said. "Maybe we ought to stick around for a while an' make sure mama lets the calf suck. Sometimes these first calf heifers will drop a calf, get up an' run around for a while then come back to the calf. Sometimes they don't come back. They're kinda scared the first time. Generally, they don't have any problems the second time they calve, they've been through it before."

"Look, he's trying it again!"

We watched as the calf tried to get to his feet. He'd make some progress, and then fall.

"It's amazing they don't hurt themselves when they fall," said Sally. "Look, he's going to try it again!"

"Their bones are still kinda soft, an' they don't weigh much now," I said.

We watched until the calf got to his feet and started looking for a teat. His balance wasn't quite right yet and he stumbled around like the drunk we'd had at the ranch last fall. But finally, he managed to find his first meal. The heifer let him suck without a problem.

"I think we can go now. We didn't have to do anything here, they're gettin' along pretty good without us. I'd better bring a horse down here tonight. If we're goin' to start calvin', we better be ready for it."

"I'll take off my saddle and leave him here," said Sally. "You were going to use him to calve anyway, weren't you? I'll ride back in the truck with you."

"I'd planned on usin' him to calve. We'll put your saddle in the back of the truck."

Sally unsaddled her horse, put her saddle in the truck and we left to finish the chores. I rode the other coming three-year-old back to the calving shed later, before supper, and checked the first calvers. Sally followed me in the truck. I left the horse and my saddle there.

At supper that night, I told Bud, "Just because you've got a painted stud, do you want everythin' on this place to have spots?"

"How's that?"

"You're goin' to have some funny lookin' calves this year," I said. "The first calf from the first calvers was born today an' he's black an' white. Kinda looks like a Holstein."

"He's not a Holstein, my boy. He's a Texas longhorn. I'm told they're supposed to be easy calvers. Did the heifer have any trouble?"

"No," I said. "I thought she was goin' to, only one foot was showin', but by the time we got her under the shed, I think every-thin' got righted an' she just had him. It was pretty easy."

"When we get a few more, I'll come down and take a look," said Bud.

"I've already got two horses down there and my saddle. I'll be gettin' up earlier to check everything in the morning, before we feed the horses. If I'm late gettin' back, it's because I've had to pull a calf, but I'll be back, sooner or later."

"Make sure you've got your electric heater Missus Aber-crombie gave you for Christmas," said Bud. "There's no heat in that little room; you might find that heater plenty handy. And don't forget, Pat can help you."

"Its already there an' bein' used," I said.

I was about to say something about Missus Abercrombie be-ing the only one thinking on the place, but decided against it. I would incriminate myself if I said anything like that.

I was glad we put electricity to the room. That heater would keep everything bearable during the winter. We didn't put wa-ter into the shed as we didn't have heat and water lines would just freeze. But there was a hydrant outside. A feller could clean up when he had to, and then dry off inside the room. I made a mental note to bring some paper towels to the calving shed the next morning.

I was up earlier the next day and drove to the calving shed. There weren't any new calves on the ground, but there were some more heifers springing. I thought I would leave the spring-ing heifers in the big pens and bring them in as they got closer to giving birth. It was hard to tell sometimes, first calf heifers could spring for quite a few days.

I went back to the ranch and helped with the chores. I thought I'd check the heifers at noon and again toward evening when I fed. The days were getting longer but there were more chores to do with the heifers starting to calve.

At noon, I went back to the calving shed and found two new calves on the ground. They were up and apparently had sucked. I saddled a horse and moved the two new mothers and their calves out of the big pens into another pen. I thought it would be easier to separate those that had calved from those that hadn't, even though it meant more chores every day, having to feed a separate pen.

That evening, I moved the springing heifers into individual pens under the calving shed. Two of the heifers had surprised me earlier and I didn't want any more to surprise me. I wanted to be ready.

The next few days went by without anything out of the ordinary happening. A few calves were born each day and up to this point I hadn't had to pull one. Then, one day a heifer was trying to deliver a calf in the breach position. I got the heifer under the shed, got the calf pullers and went to work. It was a very difficult delivery, but not before I witnessed the calf's final kicks as the umbilical cord broke and the calf took his first breath. But it wasn't a breath of air; it was a deep breath of amniotic fluid. I managed to get the rest of the calf out, but it was too late. The calf drowned with his head inside his mother.

I went to the shed and got some paint and marked the heifer. If she couldn't raise a calf, her future was sealed.

I explained to Bud what had happened at noon.

"We won't have a hundred percent calf crop this year," I said. "I lost a calf this morning."

"What happened?"

"Breech," I said. "I did all I could, but couldn't." I was bothered by the incident.

"Don't let it bother you, Honey. It's tough to get a hundred percent calf crop on any outfit. We've done pretty good so far. Do you think if I went to the sale and bought a day-old calf, we could graft it onto the heifer?"

"I'm disappointed," I said. "I've never had a perfect calving record. Looks like I won't get one this year. We could try grafting a calf on the heifer. When's the next sale?"

"Tomorrow," said Bud. "There's always next year for a hundred percent. If we can graft a calf onto the heifer, we'll still get pretty close to a hundred percent."

"I guess if we're goin' to get that heifer to adopt a calf, I better milk her out a little tonight. Maybe I ought to take a bed to the calvin' shed an' camp there. I do have heat there, an' I'd be closer in case somethin' happens," I said.

"I think you're doing all you can," said Bud. "There's no need for that. And milk the heifer out. That's a good idea."

That night, after we'd completed our feeding chores, I went to the calving shed, put the heifer in the squeeze chute and milked her out. Sally came with me.

When I was done, I asked her, "Do you want to save this milk? It's the colostrum; it might help the calf Bud gets at the sale."

"Good idea," said Sally. "We'll put it in the fridge. I'll bring a hot plate and a bottle down tomorrow, in case we need it. We can't feed it cold."

"We're goin' to have a regular nursery here if we ain't careful," I said.

"Well, isn't that the idea?"

"You're right."

The next day, Bud bought a calf from the sale and brought it to the calving pens. It was a Holstein. Sally and I put the heifer in the chute and let the calf suck, then put them both in a small pen, hoping the heifer would accept the calf. It didn't look like she would, so we separated them for the night.

Bud took his first look at his Texas longhorn crosses. "They do make for a colorful herd of calves," he said. "I don't think the buyers will pay as much for them as the straight Herford's. We'll have to separate them at sale time. Maybe we can sell them to a roping club or something. I sure hope this idea pays off."

The next morning we caught the heifer in the chute again, let the calf suck and smeared the calf's rear end with some of the colostrum milk we had saved. We also smeared a lot on the nose of the heifer. We thought if we could get the calf smelling like the heifer, she might accept the calf easier. We turned the calf and heifer into a small pen and watched them for about twenty minutes. It didn't look like the heifer was going to fight the calf. We left to do the rest of the morning chores, planning on returning before noon to see if the heifer was going to let the calf suck.

When we returned, things looked good. We decided to wait around just to see if the heifer let the calf suck. So far, things were going well. After a few days, the heifer appeared to accept the calf. We kept the new mother and her adopted calf in the small pen for a few more days, just to make sure.

I did have to pull a few calves, with results better than the first one. I was still disappointed with myself that I had lost one and was determined not to lose another one. I put all the heifers I saw springing in the smaller pens.

I did have a calf born dead and there wasn't anything I could do about it. The next sale was the following week and Sally and I milked out the heifer every day until Bud could buy another calf to put on her. It was a little more difficult to graft this calf onto the heifer than the first one, but we finally succeeded.

"I think we need to keep this pair close to the ranch this summer, or we'll end up with a leppy calf," I said. "I'm not so sure that heifer is going to take care of that calf."

"We can do that easy enough," said Sally. "We'll keep them close, maybe with Matilda and Einstein, and let the guests see them."

"Are you goin' to make a pettin' zoo?"

"No," answered Sally, "but that's an idea. We might have to take that under consideration in the future."

"Let's not take it under serious consideration," I said. "We've got plenty to do already. And remember, we still don't know what Bud's condition is. He may or may not be able to help as much as he wants to. Have you heard anything?"

"No." Sally's reply was short.

"Nothing at all?"

"If the doctor has called, Daddy hasn't said anything. If that's the case, it can't be good news. I'll question him again tonight, although I don't think it will do any good."

"Let me know if you find out anything," I said.

"Most assuredly, most assuredly," replied Sally.

Sally drilled Bud after supper that night about his condition, but without success. This only contributed to Sally's concern. I was concerned also. The only ones that didn't seem upset at the situation were Pat and Missus Abercrombie. I wondered if they knew something we didn't.

I continued checking the heifers every day. Almost all the heifers were calved out and the calves made an interesting sight—all sorts of colors and combinations of colors. They certainly didn't make for a uniform calf crop like the Herford's that had been raised on the ranch in years past.

"We'll have to sort those calves from the rest of the calves when we sell this fall," said Bud. "Buyers like uniform calf crops with regard to size, weight, and colors. But they do make an interesting sight, don't they?"

"Yep," said Pat. "There's plenty of color. Do you want to keep any of them heifers for replacements?"

"I don't think so," said Bud. "We might have enough cattle without keeping any replacements this year. Remember, we got a few more heifers from Honey's dad than what we actually needed."

"That's right," replied Pat. "But how many of them first calvers are going to rebreed?"

"Let's hope all of them. If the feed is good enough, they should. They've all had an extra thirty days or so to get back in shape," said Bud.

"What about your facility for artificially breedin' the replacement heifers? You can't afford to let it sit idle for a year; it cost too much to build. I think we need to keep at least thirty or forty heifers for replacements."

I had been listening to this conversation and said, "That sounds like a good idea to me."

"It is," said Bud, "but I might not be able to help out with this leukemia I've got."

"So that's it," I said. "Does Sally know? And how will it affect you?"

"Sally doesn't know," replied Bud. "And I'd appreciate it if you didn't tell her. With regard as to how it will affect me ..."

"Sally needs to know," I interrupted. "She has more of a right to know than anyone else!"

"Maybe you're right, Honey. I just didn't want her to worry."

"Didn't want her to worry! Why she's worried herself sick!" I was surprised at my interruption of Bud. He was my boss and I didn't do such things. "You need to tell her what's goin' on an' the sooner the better. Now, what can we expect of you?"

I thought I was exerting some authority I didn't have, but this was serious.

"Well, perhaps you're right, Honey. I can expect to lose muscle control and eventually have to use a cane, then two canes, then perhaps crutches, and eventually a wheel chair. I'll probably have to use a mounting block to get on my horse."

"You probably ought to be usin' one now," said Pat, grinning.

"Go to blazes," said Bud. "I guess I'll have to talk to Sally tonight. Now she's the only one that doesn't know. I suppose we ought to look for another year-round man while we're hiring for the summer help. I don't know that I'll be much help."

"That would be a good idea," said Pat.

That night Bud told Sally about his condition. Sally wasn't surprised. Missus Abercrombie had already told her.

"Nobody can keep a secret around here," exclaimed Bud.

"It was only proper," said Missus Abercrombie, in defense of her actions. "She should have been the first one to know! Besides that, everyone could see something was wrong. They just didn't know what!"

New Help

We still had a few heifers to calve out when the older cows started calving. The days were getting longer and we seemed to be getting busier. The older cows were dropping calves, a few every day. Pat and I were riding through the older cows every day, just checking, and I checked the first calvers every morning, noon, and night. A few of the cows needed a little help and we took them to the calving barn. We had one cow that had prolapsed and took her to the calving shed to sew her up.

As the cows calved, we'd move those that had calves into a separate pasture. When we'd get around fifty pairs, we'd move them into new pastures. Then, as the summer progressed, we could have the dudes help gather each pasture and do the branding. Almost every week we could have a branding and almost all the guests would have a chance to participate. I think that's why Sally was such a good roper—she could practice all summer long.

Bud had placed an ad for hired help in the local paper and had advertised at the state college for summertime help. We needed some maids and another wrangler. We also needed someone to help in the kitchen—the cook was slowing down. We also might need another year-round person. A few phone calls came in answering the ad and Bud made arrangements to have the applicants come out for an interview.

Sally and I were invited to attend the interviews, as, in Bud's words, "We would have to work with whoever we hired, and it was important that we all get along."

One applicant showed up driving an old pickup truck. He wasn't too clean and needed a shave. He was applying for the year-round position. He looked familiar to me, but I couldn't place where I had seen him before.

Bud had the guy fill out an application and conducted the interview, asking the customary questions: "What is your horse experience?" and "Do you drink and how much?" and "Have you ever been in jail?"

The guy had quite a bit of horse and cattle experience, he'd been a cowboy all his life. When asked if he drank, he replied, "I like a beer every now and then."

When asked if he'd ever been in jail, his reply was a short, "No."

I didn't ask any questions, trying to remember where I had seen the guy before. It bothered me that I couldn't place him, but I was sure I had met up with him.

Bud concluded the interview saying, "We're not going to hire until the first part of May. We still need to talk to a lot of people and we'll make a decision during the end of April. If you're selected, we'll get a hold of you."

The guy left and Bud turned to Sally and me. "What do you think of him?"

"I wasn't impressed," said Sally. "He needed a shave and he was very dirty. I wouldn't hire him."

"But his work experience is more than adequate," replied Bud. "I know some of these outfits he's worked for. He's got more experience than anybody we've talked to so far. What do you think Honey?"

"I ain't sure," I said. "I've seen him someplace before, but I don't know where. I don't have a good feelin' about him an' tend to agree with Sally. I don't think I'd hire him until I can figure out where I'd seen him before."

"Well, we'll just sit on this for a while. I'm not ready to make a decision yet. You let me know where you've seen him before, Honey. Maybe it was at a rodeo or in jail," said Bud, grinning.

"I ain't never been in jail," I said. Then it came to me. "But he has!"

"What? He said he'd never been to jail," said Bud.

"He lied," I said. "He's been to jail for drunk drivin' an' stealin' my horse an' donkey a couple of years ago at the rodeo. I'd got hurt an' went to the doc's an' while I was gone him an' some other guy loaded my animals in his truck an' took off with 'em. The sheriff had taken me to the doc's an' when we got back to the fairgrounds my stock was missin'. The sheriff got on the radio an' found out a highway patrolman had pulled 'em over for drunk drivin'."

I hadn't thought about the incident for some time, but I remembered the incident clearly even though it had been some years earlier, and I was a hundred percent sure this applicant was the culprit.

"I don't know why he's still not in jail," I said. "He pleaded guilty in court an' I didn't even have to go to court to testify."

"Well," said Bud, crumpling the applicant's application and depositing it in the wastebasket, "that's one we don't have to worry about. If he can't get a good reference from one of our own hired hands, we don't need him here! And if he'll lie to me about jail time, he'll lie to me about anything. We don't need him around here."

"What was his name? I might want to remember it."

"His name is Crawford," replied Bud. "George Crawford."

We had a few married people apply, but we had to turn them down as we didn't have facilities for couples. The positions provided room and board, but it was a bunkhouse living situation.

Bud made arrangements to go to the state university to interview the college students that might be interested in working for the summer. He'd talked to the school's employment counselors and set up a day to conduct interviews.

"You'll have to come with me, daughter," he told Sally. "I've come to value your opinion with regard to a lot of these matters. You got us some real fine help the last couple of years, getting Linda, Josie, and Marie. They were real good girls, and two of them worked for us for two years, but I don't think they'll be back. I know Marie won't; she's married. We'll be gone three days—a day up there, a day interviewing, and a day back."

The Wedding

Sally hadn't been riding with Pat and me for a few days. She and Missus Abercrombie had been busy planning the wedding. A date had been selected, the fifteenth of May. I didn't know what the significance of that date was, but whatever was decided was okay with me. Sally explained her plans at supper one night.

"We'll have the wedding horseback, out in the front of the lodge. Even the preacher will be horseback. It will be a small wedding, Honey's folks, you folks, and the hired help, if they want to come. We're doing it in the middle of May so we can go on a honeymoon for a week and be back before Memorial Day, when the guests start arriving. Daddy, you get to give me away."

"I always thought I'd walk you down the isle when you got married. How can I do that horseback? I suppose I'll have to lead your horse for you!"

"Fat chance," answered Sally. "I can ride my own horse!"

"Where are you goin' for a honeymoon? Niagara Falls? That's supposed to be a real popular place for honeymooners," said Pat.

"I thought we'd go south," replied Sally.

"South! There's nothing down there to do or see. What do you want to go south for?"

"We're going horseback," answered Sally. "There's plenty to see horseback."

"Horseback! That's no way to go on a honeymoon!" Bud was a little surprised at this thought. "I was prepared to let you take the company car and go wherever you wanted."

"We're going horseback, aren't we Honey." Sally was adamant about this.

I just nodded my head in agreement. This was all new to me.

"We'll take that big tent in the barn, Matilda, some groceries, and go for a couple of days," continued Sally. "We won't be too far away. I have a special spot in mind down south."

"Well," said Bud, "If that's what you really want, I guess I can't change it."

"I've already sent out invitations to Honey's folks and invited them to stay here. I've also sent invitations to Uncle Rod and Uncle Fred. We'll have the ceremony about two in the afternoon," continued Sally. "The cook can have a barbeque ready, we'll all eat, Honey and I can change clothes and then pack Matilda and we'll go. You folks can do whatever you want after that."

"Are you really in favor of this, Honey?"

"It sounds kinda like fun to me," I said. "Campin' out under the stars, sleepin' on the cold, hard ground, tryin' to get a fire goin' while I'm shiverin' in the mornin'—it's goin' to be a blast!"

Bud gave me a funny look.

Sally said, "I'm glad you like the idea, Honey. It will be a lot of fun."

Then it was my turn to give Sally a funny look.

Pat asked, "What are you goin' to do if it rains?"

"It wouldn't dare rain on my wedding day," answered Sally. "But if it does, we'll just ride into the barn and do it there!"

Pat asked, "Are we goin' to have to dress up for this?"

"It's going to be real informal," answered Sally. "I'm going to wear my mother's wedding gown. Missus Abercrombie has taken it in a little. Everyone else can wear blue jeans, maybe sport coats for the fellers."

"I don't have a sport coat," I said.

"Then you'll have to go to town and get one," ordered Sally.

"A tie, too?"

"Yes, a tie."

"I guess I'll have to get a new white shirt," I said.

"Yes!"

There was no doubt in my mind that I'd have to buy some new clothes for this occasion.

"I might as well get some new pants, too," I said.

"That would be nice," replied Sally. "I've also hired a professional photographer. You will look nice for him. He'll be the only one on foot at the wedding. He says he can get better pictures on foot."

March passed and April arrived. We were about done calving, but still feeding part of the cows. Our chores became fewer and we spent more time moving the cattle into their pastures.

"This seems like a lot of extra work to me," I said to Pat, as we moved about fifty pairs into a new pasture.

"It is," replied Pat. "But it takes a lot of the pressure off each pasture and it gives the dudes something to do—gather each pasture, brand, an' then move the cows around. It's a different form of rotating pastures. It's worked for us for a number of years.

"Tomorrow we'll run in the saddle horses and start usin' them so we won't have any surprises when the dudes arrive. Then we'll push the broodmare bunch back to their own range. We can get another look at the colt crop, even though we've seen them every day we've fed. I always like lookin' at the new colts. Bud an' Sally will probably want to come along. We might keep the broodmare bunch in and brand the colts—I'll have to talk to Bud.

"You gettin' nervous about the approachin' big day?"

I thought I'd have a little fun with Pat. "You mean when the dudes arrive?"

"No, stupid! I mean the weddin' day!"

"Not really," I said. "It's still a long time off. I need to keep busy until then so I don't get nervous."

"Yeah," said Pat. "I'll pack Matilda for you after the ceremony so you can make a quick getaway."

"Don't be tyin" no cans or anything to our horses' tails. We don't need any rodeos," I said.

"Surely, surely," said Pat, grinning.

The way he was smiling made me believe he had something else in mind and I thought I'd better keep an eye on him.

The next day, we brought the broodmare bunch in and branded the colts, then took them to their summer range. Bud and Sally helped, even though Bud had to use the mounting block to get on his big paint horse.

"My condition is getting worse faster than I expected," he said, after he got on his horse. "I might not be able to ride much longer. I don't know how much help I can be this year."

A few days later, Bud and Sally left for the university to interview students for possible summer employment. I would have liked to have gone, but there was still too much to do every day at the ranch.

While they were gone, Pat and I corralled the saddle horses and started riding them. Pat was careful to warn me about the horses that might buck during their first ride of the year.

When they returned, they'd hired three maids and two wranglers. They would be arriving the third week in May. They also had a helper for the cook, and a bunch of applications from applicants that they couldn't make up their mind about.

"Look these over," said Bud, as he handed me the applications. "We still need one more wrangler, so pick the one that looks the best to you. Take a couple of days."

A few days later Bud came to me and asked, "Have you picked a new wrangler?"

"I sorta settled on one feller," I said.

"Well," said Bud. "Forget him. Jim, the guy that's kinda been our head housekeeper the last couple of years, he called and wants to come back. I hired him and at Sally's suggestion, we don't need another wrangler. She's going to do the job."

"That's good," I said. "She can do a better job than anyone we might hire."

We continued riding the dude horses, giving the horses we'd used all winter a well-deserved break. My saddle horse, Roman, had wintered well and he didn't offer to buck during his first ride.

When the first of May arrived, we only had three cows that hadn't calved. We put them in the calving sheds and would only have to check on them in the morning and feed them in the evening. We could use the dude horses to do that as we were riding them every day. We made ready to start breeding the replacement heifers. The inseminator arrived and we provided him with a place to stay.

The plan was that the inseminator would ride the pens in the morning and evening looking for the bullers. Bullers are heifers that are riding other heifers or standing to be ridden. A cow, or heifer, coming into heat will ride others for about twelve hours, in heat they'll stand to be ridden for about twelve hours and if they aren't bred, they ride others for about twelve hours.

The bullers that were pulled the night before and the bullers that were pulled in the morning would be bred in the afternoon. The plan was for me to help pull the bullers every day.

"When are you goin' to town to get some new weddin' clothes? I might need to go with you an' pick out some new duds for myself," said Pat.

"I dunno," I said. "Whenever it's convenient. You can ride along with me if you want. We've got to do it pretty soon, the big day is arriving."

"We better do it tomorrow," he said, "while we're thinkin' about it."

At supper that night, Pat told Bud, "Honey an' me are goin' to town to get some weddin' duds tomorrow. We'll get the chores done early an' be back early, if you don't mind."

"That sounds good to me," said Bud.

"But not to me," said Sally. "I don't think it's a good idea to let you guys go to town alone. There's no telling what you'll come back with or what you'll look like at the wedding! I'm going with you!"

"How can we give Honey a bachelor party with you along?"

"He doesn't need one," answered Sally. "Really, Pat, I think there's a little bit of the devil in you."

The next day Sally, Pat, and I went to town. We didn't bother going to the department store, we went to the western wear store.

"How's this look?" I was holding up a gaudy-looking sport coat.

"I knew I came along for a reason," said Sally.

"Darlin', I was only teasin'."

"I'll bet! If I'd have let you guys come alone, you'd look like a couple of clowns at my wedding. Does this fit?" She handed me a solid-colored sport coat.

"Do you like it?" I tried it on. "It fits."

"And it looks good on you. Do you like it?"

"I've never had anything like this before. I guess it's all right. If you like it, I'll get it," I said. "Now, how about a wide-striped shirt to go with it?"

"No," said Sally. "I don't want you looking like an escaped convict at my wedding!"

I got a plain white shirt, and a black western tie. A new pair of Levis and a new hat completed my shopping. I was ready to get back to the ranch.

Pat didn't get any help from Sally picking out his new clothes, but she was watching at the checkout counter.

"Do my selections meet your approval?"

"Yes," answered Sally. "You did very well, much better than my future husband. I might have to dress him every day in the future."

Pat just laughed.

As we started out of town, I had one more stop—the jewelry store. I hadn't got a wedding band!

Pat stayed in the truck while Sally and I went in the store. "Pick out something you like," I said, "but don't make it too expensive. Remember, I'll have to support you in the future!"

Sally picked out a band, I paid for it and after we got something to eat, we headed for the ranch. I always felt relieved when I left town, I don't know why, I just didn't feel comfortable in towns.

When we got back to the ranch, we found that the remaining three cows that hadn't calved had.

"I had to pull one," said Bud, "and lost him. A few years ago I could have done it without any problem, but I can't now. I guess I'm losing my strength. I'll go to the sale tomorrow and get a day-old calf we can graft onto the cow. We'll have to milk out the cow tonight."

"Is that why I got a new set of clothes, so I can milk out a cow?" I was trying to be funny. Bud laughed. Sally didn't.

"Don't be silly, stupid! You got new clothes so you could marry me!"

"Oh," I said.

That night after supper, Pat and I had a discussion in the bunkhouse. "I don't think we should leave the ranch together again," he said.

"How come?"

"Bud's startin' to lose it. Not his mind, but he's goin' downhill fast physically. If he continues to insist on ridin', we might have to have someone accompany him everywhere."

Three days before the wedding, my family showed up. It was good to see them again, as I hadn't seen them for about a year. Sally and my mother had a very warm greeting and I was glad they got along well.

At supper the conversation was mostly about the wedding.

My dad asked, "Who's going to be your best man, son?"

"Well," I said, "seein' as I'm the one gettin' married, it only figures that I'm the best man!"

"That ain't right," said Sally.

"Isn't," corrected Missus Abercrombie.

"I was thinkin' either Pat or Tommy," I said.

"You take your brother," said Pat. "I'll have plenty to do."

After supper, my dad and Bud discussed the cattle business, Sally and my mom discussed the wedding, and I took Tommy and Betty to the horse corrals and showed them Matilda and Einstein.

"Can I ride Matilda at the wedding?" My sister had a particular liking for the burros. "I rode Sassy for the parade!"

"No," I said. "We've got a special horse for you."

A day later, Rod and Fred, Bud's brothers, showed up. Fred brought his family—four kids and their mom. Rod rode his horse; he didn't own a car or truck.

I thought when I saw the kids, mostly teenagers, "The tourist season has started early." But they were all horse people and we didn't have to give any instructions as to riding.

The day of the wedding arrived. Everyone was up early to get the chores done. When we were done with the chores, I went to brushing and saddling the horses. Sally wasn't to be seen.

The last horse I saddled was Roman. I did a particularly good job of brushing him. This was Sally's day and I wanted everything to be just right for her. After I got Roman cleaned up,

I went to the bunkhouse, got out my new clothes, and proceeded to clean up myself.

At 1:30, I left the bunkhouse, figuring on helping get everyone mounted. Much to my surprise, everyone was already mounted. I looked around and couldn't see Sally or Bud.

The photographer had each family pose for pictures on their horses. When my family posed, my dad asked, "Are you nervous son?"

"About like the first time I got on a saddle bronc at my first rodeo," I said.

"That's natural. I know I was really scared when I married your mom."

Mother gave him a dirty look and Dad quickly added, "But I'm glad I went through with it!"

"Tommy," I said, as I handed him the ring, "you take this, don't lose it and give it to me when the time comes."

He took the ring and put it half way on one of his fingers.

"Put it in your pocket, dummy!"

"I won't forget where it is here," he replied.

The preacher was in place on his horse, and he instructed me as to where to put my horse. Tommy rode up beside me. I still couldn't see Sally.

Presently, Sally and Bud came riding out from behind the lodge. Bud was riding his big paint and Sally was on her grulla. Even from a distance, she made a pretty picture. They rode slowly toward the gathering. As they approached us, Bud told everyone, "She looks just like her mother."

The cook left his barbeque and joined the group next to Pat.

Bud brought Sally up beside me and turned his horse away.

"You sure look pretty," I whispered to Sally.

"And you look grand," she replied.

I touched Roman with a spur and he side-passed up next to the grulla. The preacher began.

At the proper time, Tommy got the ring off his finger and gave it to me without dropping it, thank goodness.

The preacher ended the ceremony with, "You may now kiss the bride."

As Sally leaned over to kiss me and I leaned over to kiss her, the grulla shied and jumped away. Sally touched him with her heel and the horse promptly stepped back. Before she kissed me, Sally said, "I need to do a better job of training this horse!"

We turned our horses toward the people and accepted their congratulations.

The cook said, "Whoever wants their food well done better come now. If you don't, it'll be burnt."

Everyone turned their horses toward the barn, rode over and turned them loose in the corral. Sally and I tied our horses at the hitch rail alongside the barn, and went to the lodge to eat. As we walked to the lodge, I noticed Bud. He was using the mounting block to get off his horse.

We ate a hearty meal. Unbeknownst to us, the cook had baked a three-layer cake and put a couple of plastic cowboys on horses on it. We cut the cake and Sally gave me the first piece, smearing a good part of it all over my face. I started to wipe it off with my sleeve, but my mother shoved a Kleenex in my hand.

"Here," she said.

Presently, Pat showed up. He walked up beside me, kissed Sally and shook my hand. "Your burro is packed," he said. "I tied her down by your horses. You can go any time. By the way, put a dried cow chip on the fire before you go to bed. It'll smolder all night an' it'll be easier to get a fire goin' in the mornin'."

We posed for more pictures and before we left to change clothes, she raised her dress, took off her garter and tossed it to one of her cousins. I noticed that when she raised her dress, she had her cowboy boots and spurs on. "One hundred percent cowboy," I thought to myself.

With our clothes changed, we went to our horses. I was surprised. The saddle on my horse had been put on backward! Pat! I knew he'd do something. And on the rump of Sally's grulla someone had printed: "JUST MARRIED" with a red grease sheep marker, no doubt supplied by Rod.

I quickly resaddled my horse much to the amusement of the family. Sally got on her horse and I got on Roman, gathered up the lead rope Pat handed me, and we headed out, amongst the well wishes of the family.

"Some how or other," I said, "I'll get even with you, Pat!"

We headed south on our honeymoon with Sally leading the way. When we were a couple of miles away, out of sight of the lodge, we made a big circle and headed back north.

"Where we goin? Are you lost?"

"No," answered Sally. "I've got a special spot on mind."

"But I thought you said it was south an' now we're headed north."

"I just said south to confuse anybody that might want to follow us," she said.

Soon we arrived at Sally's special spot. It was the family graveyard.

"There's about ten acres fenced here," said Sally. "We can put the tent up under those trees. There's water in that little spring for us and the horses. Don't you think it's beautiful?"

"It is nice," I said. "If you're happy with it, then so am I."

I got off Roman, opened the gate and Sally rode through. I closed the gate, got back on and we rode toward the trees. At the trees, we dismounted. Sally unsaddled her horse and I tended to Matilda and Roman.

"What in the worlds goin' on? This pack is really confusing," I said. "I thought Pat was a better packer than this."

"They might be playing games with us," said Sally. "You figure that out and I'll hunt up some firewood."

I finally got Matilda's pack undone. Pat had used about seventy-five feet of rope to pack and it must have been his way of having fun. I unsaddled Roman and set about putting the tent up. I was relieved to find that it was complete. I was a little leery of what Pat might have done.

With the tent up, Sally asked me, "Aren't you going to carry me across the threshold?"

"I kinda thought your horse did that when I opened the gate for you," I said.

"Very romantic!"

Sally helped me go through the rest of the pack. There were enough canned goods to provide us with a week's worth of food, utensils, and cooking gear. There was plenty of bedding. After we'd unpacked everything, we started a fire and settled back to relax. We were on our honeymoon. I carried her over the threshold of the tent just before it began to rain. I didn't put a cow chip on the fire, knowing it would stink all night as it smoldered.

"I told you it wouldn't rain on my wedding day," said Sally.

Back to the Routine

On the last day of our honeymoon, we took down the tent, gathered up our garbage, packed Matilda, and headed back to the ranch. We had spent a week camped out and had a good time. Our horses were well rested and had put on a little more weight.

When we rode into the ranch, Bud was on the porch and greeted us. "How's the newlyweds? Liking married life?"

"Yes sir," I replied. "But I'm ready to get back to work. I've been idle too long."

"I'll bet," said Bud, smiling. "You can move your stuff up here. I'm giving you my living quarters, I've already moved into another room."

"But we don't want to disrupt you," I said.

"It's not a disruption," answered Bud. "You'll have your own bedroom, an office, and your own bathroom. We've already put your wedding gifts in there, thanks to Missus Abercrombie. There's even a TV in there. It's way too big for me alone. After supper, I want to talk to you kids about the future of this ranch. Now take care of your animals and bring your stuff from the bunkhouse up here. This is your home now. Be ready to start work tomorrow, there are already some dudes ... er ... guests here—two families. I saw an opportunity to make a little extra cash and decided to take it. Missus Abercrombie has made them comfortable so far."

We put our horses and Matilda away.

"I'd better go get acquainted with our guests," said Sally. "You can move your stuff into our new house."

As I was moving my stuff into the house, I noticed a funny-looking vehicle at the side of the lodge.

At supper, I asked Bud about the little cart alongside the lodge.

"That's a golf cart," said Bud.

"You goin' to take up golf?"

"No, but I'm going to use it to get around. I'm having trouble getting on my horse. And if I get off somewhere, I might not be able to get back on. Now," continued Bud, "about the future of this ranch."

I could tell Bud didn't like talking about his condition.

He continued, "We're going to continue raising cattle, horses, and taking in dudes. Sally, I'm going to let you handle the dude part of the operation. I'll handle the phone and reservations while you're out horseback. You've been around it and have been doing more of it than you realize. And you're good with the people, especially the kids. You'll make a great mother when the time comes, just like your own mother.

"Honey, you're going to be foreman. You'll be in …"

"I think Pat ought to have that job," I interrupted. "He's been here longer than I have an' already knows more about what's goin' on than I do."

"Pat doesn't want the job," answered Bud. "I've already spoken to him about it. He's content to continue doing just as he has been doing. But as foreman, you listen to him, like you say, he knows what's going on. I don't think you'll have to tell him much about what you want him to do, he knows the routine. Honey, you'll be in charge of the horse and cattle aspect of the ranch. You two kids will have to work together in the overall management of this ranch. I'm turning it over to you, but I'll be around if you need to get some expert advice." Bud smiled as he made the last comment.

"I've made out a new will …"

Sally interrupted, "Daddy! What do you mean?" She was very concerned.

"I mean, daughter, I've made out a new will. You two are now my sole beneficiaries. In the event of my death, you will inherit the ranch. In the new will, I've given Pat, the cook, and Virginia, that is Missus Abercrombie, a lifetime tenancy here on this ranch. They can quit working whenever they want to and still stay here free of charge. Of course, Missus Abercrombie doesn't really work, but she's been real helpful in the past. They'll be free to do anything they want to as long as it doesn't interfere with the normal ranch operations. Is that understood?"

Sally and I agreed.

"I think you ought to put Sally in charge of the finances," I said. "My math ain't too good."

"I'm going to put both of you on the checking account. I'll stay on it, of course. But you'll need to be on it, Honey. You'll need to buy some more bulls next spring and it will be handy for brand inspections and the like. I'll fill Sally in with the monthly payments and such. I got some signature cards from the bank when I bought the golf cart. Here, both of you sign them. I'll take them to the bank next trip to town."

He handed the signature cards to us.

"Now, Honey, I've written down about when we can expect to brand during the summer. If it rains, you'll have to reschedule. By the way, did you get wet on your honeymoon?"

"No," I answered. "We got everything set up before the rain came."

"I know," said Bud.

"How did you know, Daddy?"

"After the ceremony and everyone left, I went up there to be with your mother. You're married now, and your mother's memory is all I have left."

"Oh Daddy!" Sally got up and went to Bud and gave him a big hug, with tears starting to form in her eyes.

"I'm not really gone, Daddy. You know I'll always be here. How come you didn't come to our camp?"

"Don't be like that, daughter," said Bud, brushing her away. "I didn't come to your camp because it was your honeymoon and you needed to be alone. But I'm glad you shared it with your mother, though. You remember the stories I used to tell you when you were a little girl, don't you?"

"Oh yes," Daddy. "How could I ever forget them?"

"It's getting late now, you kids need to go to bed. I'm going to turn in myself," said Bud. "Oh, by the way, Sally, you better start riding my big paint horse. I'm giving him to you as a wedding present. I can hardly get on him anymore. And, before I forget it, I'm giving you both a raise. I can't have my daughter living close to poverty on this ranch. Consider it another wedding present!"

The next day, I was up early. Pat and Sally and I ran the saddle horses in. On the way to breakfast, I asked Pat about how felt about the changes with me being foreman.

"I don't think we'll have any problems," he said. "You seem to know what's goin' on. If I'd have known you was goin' to be my boss, I might have tied that pack on better an' not put your saddle on your horse backward."

We both laughed. "You know I'll get even some day, don't you? How come you don't want the foreman job?"

"To be honest, this place don't really need a foreman. We take care of the livestock in the winter an' we take care of the dudes in the summer. It's pretty simple, unless we hire a complete idiot. Then we'll have to tell him an' probably show him how to do it. When it comes to that, we'll have more work."

"You're right there," I said.

At breakfast, I met the new guests. Sally's introduction went, "Honey, meet the Zimmermans, Dan and Polly, and the Stanfords, Steve and Margo. This is my husband, Honey. They have a lot in common with us, they're newlyweds, on their honeymoon."

"Honey! What's his real name?"

"I've answered to Honey ever since I got here," I said. "I think its Sally's idea of a joke."

"There'll be a lot of confusion around here with everyone answering to Honey."

"Yes, there will be," came the reply in unison. I even joined in with them.

"We understand you just got off your honeymoon," said Dan. "Where did you go?"

"We stayed right here on the ranch," said Sally. "It was very romantic. We camped out."

"You mean he didn't even carry you across the threshold?"

"He told me my horse did that when he opened the gate," said Sally.

"Oh brother," said Polly.

I was beginning to feel my face getting flushed. "Let's go for a ride. What kind of riders are you?"

Margo said, "That really sounds romantic to me, camping out. We should try that, Steve. That sounds like it was fun. We haven't done much riding,"

"We haven't done much either," said Polly.

"I'll get some real gentle horses caught an' saddled," I said. "We'll take a real easy ride an' check some fences."

Pat was already at the corral when I got there. He had some gentle horses saddled, and then went about saddling his own horse. I saddled Drygulch for me and Sally saddled Bud's big paint. As the Zimmermans and Stanfords arrived, Pat was just getting on his horse.

When Pat moved his horse out, the horse bogged his head and started to buck. Pat let him go a few jumps, then pulled up his head. He trotted the horse around the corral then urged him into a slow lope. When he got done, he rode the horse over to the gate, got off and led the horse up to Polly.

"You're horse is ready for you now, ma'am," he said, handing the reins to Polly.

"I'm not riding that horse," exclaimed Polly, backing away from Pat. Everyone else was laughing.

"No ma'am," said Pat, "I'm just kidding. Your horse is over here. We call him Sleepy. He's plumb gentle."

"Then you get on him first," said Polly.

Pat got Sleepy and stepped up on him. He rode him around in a circle. "See, he's real gentle."

After some coaxing from Dan, she got on. Pat helped her and adjusted her stirrups. Then he gave her some pointers on neck reining. While he was doing this, Sally and I got everyone else mounted and got on our own horses.

"Let's ride" said Sally, and started out. The Zimmermans and Stanfords followed. "We'll go slow and enjoy the scenery."

We left the ranch and started toward the west side. There were a lot of trees west of us and Sally had picked one of the most scenic trails we had for an hour or so ride.

I rode up to Sally to take my customary position in front, but Sally wouldn't give up the lead position. "You go back and talk to the folks," she said.

I asked, "Are you still working on my social graces?"

"No," she answered, "but you are!"

We rode for about an hour and a half, ending up back at the barn. I had tried to make small talk with the guests but without much success, although Margo did ask me if it were possible if she and her husband could go camping out.

I told her, "We really don't do that, but it might be arranged. I'll look into it."

I was really glad Pat was along; he filled in the blank spots very nicely.

Both the Zimmermans and Stanfords were a little saddle sore when we got back and headed right for their cabins. The thought of an afternoon sunbathing and swimming in the pool would be comforting to them.

"Do you want to take Margo an' Steve campin'? We could do it real easy, take 'em up on the mountain, leave 'em an' come back an' get 'em in a couple days. It would be just like a drop camp," I said.

"I don't really think it's a good idea," said Sally. "We've always kept the guests here at the ranch. It's easier to supervise them and keep them out of trouble. We can try it if you want to."

"I suppose if we let them camp, we'd have to come out an' check up on them every day."

"That's right," said Sally. "And they'd have to do their own cooking. There's no telling what might happen."

"I'll tell 'em we can't," I said.

I discussed the camping idea with Steve and Margo after supper that night, explaining that it was highly irregular, and it was not a part of what we normally offered. I tried to suggest that it might even be a little dangerous. I concluded by saying, "In your own best interests, I don't think we should even attempt it."

Margo was very disappointed but Steve didn't seem too disappointed. He actually looked a little relieved.

I told Sally about the encounter with Steve and Margo and that the matter was settled. I also added, "It might not be a good idea to tell everyone we honeymooned on the ranch, campin' out. It might suggest that we'll allow campin' for anybody."

Sally agreed. "You're getting to know the dude aspect of this operation pretty well. I'll have to be more careful of what I say in front of the dudes. You won't have to worry much, you don't say much to start with."

"I do answer questions when asked," I said, in self-defense.

"True," answered Sally. "You're still my silent, bashful cowboy. Don't ever change.

"Our new hired help should be arriving any day now. You'll have to be in charge of training our new wranglers with regard to our procedures. I'll help train the household staff along with Jim and Missus Abercrombie. Our first scheduled guests should be arriving Friday or Saturday. Are you ready?"

"I think so," I said, although I was always apprehensive when new guests showed up."

A few days later, the new hired help showed up. The first to arrive was the cook's helper, a feller named Jacob. Then Jim, the head housekeeper arrived. He had worked here for the previous two years, and already knew what to do. His presence would make Sally's job easier, and she would be able to spend more time horseback with the dudes and cattle. The new maids showed up and finally the new wranglers.

There were two new wranglers from the state university, both majoring in animal husbandry. One of them had an extra large belt buckle on that signified his having won a bull-dogging contest. This guy was big and he had a lot of muscle. His name was Jason.

The other guy, Richard, was smaller, more about my size. He was ranch raised and was going to school to further his education so he could run his parent's ranch when he graduated.

To me, it looked like we wouldn't have to do much training with these new hired hands. A little familiarization with our procedures and we would be set. The main thing with new help was to train them to keep an eye on the dudes and prevent any mishaps from happening before they did. Safety was a big consideration with the dudes along with the safety of the hired help.

The following morning, Sally, Pat, Jason, Richard, and I saddled horses and rode out to gather the broodmare band. We planned on branding the colts and taking pictures for registration purposes.

As we rode out in search of the broodmare bunch, I told Jason and Richard what was expected of them. "This isn't a straight ridin' job," I said, "although there's a lot of ridin' involved. Our main concern is keepin' the guests happy an' busy, if they want to stay busy. We're basically babysitters for tourists. There's a lot of other stuff to do, like unload the hay when it comes in. We'll need enough to feed the horses and cows and bulls all winter along with the replacement heifers.

"We don't have any irrigatin' to do, the lack of which I'm most grateful for," I continued. "When new guests arrive, we need to help them take their luggage to their room or cabin. If you see anything that needs doin', do it."

Jason asked, "Just who do we take our orders from?"

"Well," I said, "Bud's the owner. I got the title of foreman although Pat really should have it. If you have any problems or questions, come to me, or my wife Sally, an' we'll handle it. If Pat tells you to do somethin', do it. We generally get along pretty well here, without to much bossin'.

My explanations of what was expected of the hired help seemed to satisfy them and I dropped back to ride with Sally.

"I listened to your discussion with Jason and Richard," she said.

"What did you think?"

"I was quite impressed," answered Sally. "You're making great improvements in your social graces. I even noticed that you didn't refer to the guests as dudes. You've got the rest of us calling them dudes, but you're coming around."

"I'm glad you approve of my efforts," I said. "You know, the foreman on an outfit does have some responsibility when it comes to settin' an example."

Both Pat and Sally laughed.

We spotted the band shortly after arriving on their range. "Honey," said Pat, "why don't you an' Sally lead this bunch in? These boys an' I can follow."

I noticed that Pat had replaced his lariat rope with his bullwhip.

"Who are you plannin' on usin' for bait? I'd like to watch this time," I said.

Pat just smiled as we started out. "Sometimes you can't be to sure," he said.

Sally and I led the horses to the corrals at the ranch. The Stanfords and Zimmermans hadn't left yet and Bud had given them a ride to the corrals in the golf cart. He was using it more frequently now.

The broodmare band tried to turn back at the corrals. I yelled, "You folks need to step back a ways! Bud, you oughta move that golf cart back. It's spookin' these horses!" The horses had never seen a golf cart before.

The Zimmermans and Stanfords stepped out of sight into the barn. Bud drove the golf cart into the barn and we corralled the horses without any further difficulty.

Pat roped the stud and tied him outside the corral. A fire was built and we set about branding the colts. Bud had brought the camera and Sally took pictures of each side of each colt.

I hadn't had a chance to look over the colts until I had to rope them. There was a lot of color and the colts looked good. Pat and I would be halter breaking them this winter.

I was glad Jason was there. He was big enough and strong enough to be able to hold the colts against the fence without too much trouble as Pat branded them. Richard kept the irons hot and assisted with holding the colts when necessary. Bud and the guests stayed outside the corral and I could hear Bud explaining why the colts were branded and just how it was done.

When we finished the branding, we let the horses stand in the corral while Bud looked them over real close. When he was satisfied, we took the band back to their range and turned them loose.

At supper that night, we discussed the colt crop. Bud was pleased with them and was sure he could have a good sale two years down the road. Knowing he was pleased, I said, "I didn't really mean to yell at you today, but the mares wanted to turn back an' we were too close to gettin' 'em corralled, I didn't want to lose 'em."

"Don't fret on it, Honey. You were right. I should have put that golf cart out of sight long before you showed up. If you hadn't yelled, I wouldn't have moved it; I forgot all about it."

Pat laughed and asked, "Do you think the title foreman is goin' to his head? Yellin' at the owner like that. What's this younger generation comin' to anyways?"

"Well," said Bud, "he was right! If he wasn't so new to his position, he'd probably have cussed me to boot. And don't be so critical of Honey, Pat. I seem to remember a few times when you yelled at me and you didn't forget the cussing!"

They both laughed and I got the impression they had many adventures and misadventures in the past. I made a mental note to ask Pat about it in the future.

The Zimmermans and the Stanfords left the next day, and more guests arrived. We soon settled into a summer routine. We'd gather the saddle horses every morning before breakfast. At breakfast we'd find out which guests wanted to ride and then saddle their horses for them. We'd offer a couple of different rides each day of varying lengths; an hour, two hours, or three hours. There would be rides just to enjoy the scenery, and every so often we'd gather cattle and move them to a different pasture in preparation for a branding. Then, every couple of weeks, we'd take everyone and gather cattle to brand.

At the brandings, we'd give everyone a chance to rope calves, but Sally and I did most of the roping. Jason was a fair roper and could even spin a rope some. Richard couldn't catch much when he roped.

I asked him, "How come you're havin' such a hard time catchin' any calves?"

"I haven't roped much," he said. "At our ranch, we use a calf table to brand."

"A red roper," said Pat. He'd been eavesdropping on our conversation. "That takes all the skill an' fun out of brandin'. It ain't goin' to be too long that all our cowboy skills are just for show; a relic of the Old West that's just done to show how we used to do it. I don't know what the world's comin' to!"

"You're probably right, Pat," I said.

"The calf table is more efficient," said Richard. "And it causes less stress on the animal."

Occasionally, Bud would come to the brandings, arriving when we were about half done. He'd drive his golf cart over from the lodge and generally sit in the cart and just watch. He'd usually bring a thermos of cold lemonade to share with everyone. He was a welcome sight when he showed up.

Bud's condition was getting worse. Some days he would be in pretty good shape and others, he could hardly get out of bed. I watched him closely, as did Sally and Pat. We didn't openly discuss his condition, but all three of us were very concerned.

We planned on branding one day and just about had the cattle corralled when the wind came up and it started to rain. And it rained hard! Everyone got their rain jackets on, but not before they got pretty wet. I knew we couldn't brand in the rain, so I called off the branding and we headed back to the lodge.

"These calves can get branded tomorrow," I said. "We don't need to get this done in this kind of weather!"

Most of the dudes looked relieved when we were headed back. I don't think there's anything more miserable than being soaking wet in a rainstorm while horseback. When we arrived at the lodge, the cook came out to meet us.

"Did you see Bud?"

"No," I answered. "I didn't know he was comin' out today."

"He left right after you all did. You should have seen him."

"Which way did he go?" There were a number of different ways he could have gone in the golf cart.

"I don't know," said the cook. "You know how he is. He left sayin' 'I'll bet I can find the branding corrals. Of course he could find them, he helped build them when he was a kid! He's in the golf cart and he could get that stuck on a sagebrush."

"Sally," I said, "you take the company truck an' drive out to the brandin' corrals on the north side. I'll take my truck an' go out on the south side. Whoever finds him, lay on the horn, an' lay on it hard! It'll be hard to hear it in this wind and rain.

"Pat, you take care of the horses an' I'd appreciate it if you unsaddled Sally's horse an' mine. If we ain't back by the time you've done that, get the two-ton truck an' come lookin' for us. As hard as it's rainin', we both stand the chance of gettin' stuck."

Pat nodded his head in agreement and started unsaddling horses with Richard and Jason.

"I'll get some blankets from the laundry room," said Sally. "I'll bet he's soaking, ringing wet!"

Sally had already left by the time I got my truck. It was difficult to see in the rain and the storm seemed to be gaining strength. The idea of trying to pick up his tracks wasn't considered as it was raining too hard. The wind hadn't eased up either.

After about half an hour, I heard Sally's horn. She had found Bud. Now if I could find her, our hunt was over. Presently, I found Sally and Bud parked on a hill. The golf cart was tipped over on its side. Sally had managed to help Bud into the cab of the truck.

As I approached the truck, I asked, "What happened?"

"Get in out of the rain so I can roll up this window and I'll tell you," said Bud.

He slid over on the seat and I got in the cab.

"Roll up that window! Where were you born, in a barn? I'm freezing!" Bud was cold but he hadn't lost his sense of humor.

I rolled up the window. "Just what do you think you're doin' out here in a rainstorm?"

"I started to lose traction so I decided to turn around and head back. When I gunned it in reverse, the left rear wheel hit a rock and it flipped over."

"You're lucky it didn't toss you out and land on you," I said. "Are you hurt?"

"No," said Bud, "just a few scrapes. I've been tossed off better horses than that thing!"

"Sally, you head back the same way you came. I'll follow you. See if you can turn this truck around without turnin' it over." I nudged Bud in the ribs as I made the last comment, thinking it was kinda funny.

"Ouch! That's kinda tender there," cried Bud.

"Didn't mean to," I said. "How bad is it?"

"It's nothing," replied Bud.

"Sally, get goin'. I'll be right behind you. Go right up to the lodge when you get there."

On the way back, Sally asked Bud, "What do you think of the way my husband's taking charge of things?"

"I'm not surprised," answered Bud. "He hasn't shown me any less than what I expected of him and quite often he's shown me quite a bit more. He's doing what he's supposed to do. Has he lived up to your expectations?"

"Most assuredly, Father, most assuredly."

I followed Sally to the lodge and helped get Bud inside. Missus Abercrombie, the cook, and hired help were all waiting.

"Better get him in a hot bath, he's took quite a chill. We don't want him comin' down with pneumonia," I said.

Missus Abercrombie gave me a startled, surprised look, but helped Bud inside.

"I think we can call it a day, if all the chores are done," I said.

Everyone assured me the chores were done.

"Then we can get ready for supper," I said. "Remember, we still have guests to look after and we'll need an early start in the morning. We've still got calves to brand tomorrow."

As Sally and I headed upstairs to get cleaned up, I said, "Just when I was gettin' settled into the routine, somethin' like this has to happen."

"Don't be mad at Daddy for what happened, Honey. It wasn't his fault."

"I know, Darlin'. I ain't mad at your dad. But just when I think things are goin' fine, a monkey wrench gets thrown into the mix. I guess I'll just have to learn to expect the unexpected."

"Did you see the surprised look Missus Abercrombie gave you when you told someone to get Daddy into a hot bath?"

"I saw that," I said. "She hasn't looked at me like that since I first met her an' yelled at her to quit followin' that cow through the middle of the herd. It was kinda funny."

"Daddy thinks you're doing a fine job," said Sally.

"I'm just doin' what needs to be done," I said.

"That's what I love about you," said Sally. "There's not a pretentious bone in your body. I've got an idea and I think I'll have to go to town tomorrow. Do you need anything?"

"Maybe some razor blades an' some shavin' cream," I said. "What's your idea?"

"I'll let you know."

After supper I went to the bunkhouse to talk to Pat. "I didn't mean to be so bossy this afternoon," I said. "But there was an emergency. I really do appreciate you're takin' care of mine an' Sally's horses."

"That's not a problem," said Pat. "I knew something was happenin'. I noticed the old man didn't come down to supper. Is he all right?"

"I think so," I said. "After he got out of the tub, Missus Abercrombie made him get into bed an' she brought him his supper. If its still rainin' tomorrow, we'll go get the golf cart righted an' bring it home. Sally's goin' to town tomorrow, do you need anything?"

"Not really. Just some razor blades an' some shavin' cream," answered Pat. "Tell her she might look for some sort of harness an' a leash to keep Bud under control!"

We both laughed and I went back to the lodge sayin' to myself, "Great minds think along the same lines."

Bear Scare

It was still raining the next day. We gathered the saddle horses although it was doubtful any of the guests would want to ride. Bud came down for breakfast and I couldn't tell if he had a new limp or if his condition was causing him problems. Sally and Missus Abercrombie went to town right after breakfast.

Jason, Richard, and I went to get the golf cart in my truck. I thought Jason was stout enough he could probably get it righted by himself, but many hands make for light work. Richard volunteered to drive the cart back.

"You're liable to get wet," I said.

"That's all right," said Richard. "I've gotten wet before."

"You go ahead an' we'll follow," I said. "When you get to the ranch, park it behind the lodge an' plug it in. Even though the top is bent some, Bud can still use it. If you're goin' to tip it over, tip it on the other side. Maybe it will straighten out the top."

I made the last comment in jest and the small amount of humor was not lost on Richard and Jason. They both were grinning as we started for the ranch. As I followed the golf cart, I noticed Richard looking all around the inside of the cart.

"If he don't pay attention to where he's goin', he'll tip it over again," I told Jason.

Then he stopped and came back to the truck. "I'd like to take this straight to the barn," he said when he got to the truck. "I think we can straighten it out fairly easily."

"If you think you can do it," I said, "then do it. It don't look like we got much else to do today."

Richard drove straight to the barn and by noon he had the cover fairly straight. He drove the cart to the lodge for the noon meal, parked it and plugged it in. Bud came out and inspected his work.

"That's almost like new," he said. "Good job! How did you do it?"

"I just undid a couple of bolts, got a piece of pipe and straightened it out. Jason here supplied the muscle. I had a lot of time to look it over driving it back here."

"That's good!"

Later that day, Sally returned with Missus Abercrombie. I was anxious to know what Sally's idea was, as she hadn't told me anything about it before she left.

Sally brought in a sack with razor blades and shaving cream for Pat and myself. She also had a bigger sack with a large box in it.

"This is a two-way radio," she said, as she pulled the box out of the sack. "There's a base unit we'll keep in the kitchen where the cook can monitor it. There's two hand-held radios. We'll keep one with Daddy and the other one we'll take with one of us on the trail. That way, if Daddy gets into trouble, he can radio back to the cook and the cook can radio us if we don't get his call. I hope it works, it cost a pretty penny."

Pat asked, "Ain't they just communications for line of sight transmissions?"

"No," replied Sally. "They're supposed to be good anywhere for seven to ten miles. The hand-held radios will need to be charged each night. Daddy's radio we can charge at the base unit, here's a charger we can put in the barn to charge our radio."

"How are we goin' to carry them? They're to big to keep in a shirt pocket," I said. "I'd be afraid they'd fall out if I had to move my horse out of a walk."

"I can fix that," said Pat. "Let me take 'em for a spell, I'll have somethin' worked out."

Pat took one of the radios and the charger to the barn. The other radio we plugged into the charger with the base unit. We knew we had something when we plugged in the unit and the light came on. Pat plugged in the portable charger and started charging the other radio in the barn.

At supper, Pat said, "If you boys can gather the horses in the morning, I'll be about done with my project by breakfast an' we can get back into our regular routine."

"What do you mean boys? I'm going to help," said Sally.

The next morning, we gathered the saddle horses without Pat. During breakfast he came in carrying two scabbards for the two-way radios.

"You can put a radio in each one of these. One goes with the golf cart an' one we can tie on one of our saddles. We'll take 'em out today an' try 'em out. What you got lined out for today, Honey?"

"It's goin' to be too muddy to brand, maybe we can get to that tomorrow. We'll just take the dudes out sightseeing today."

We found out who wanted to ride and saddled their horses. The day was spent sightseeing from the back of a horse. Sally tried out the radio we'd brought along and it seemed to work fine. The cook had some difficulty with the transmitter, but finally figured it out.

"That's a real good idea you had, Darlin'. The only thing wrong is that we ought to have another one or two 'cause we're often separated an' its kinda inconvenient. If we're goin' to have communication, it should be total," I said.

"I got to thinking about that on the way home," said Sally,

"and came to the same conclusion. I've already asked Missus Abercrombie to pick up two more radios when she takes Daddy into town next week. With two more radios, you, Pat, and I can each carry one. That should be enough."

"It's goin' to be difficult to remember to plug 'em in each night," I said. "What's Bud goin' to town for?"

"True, but it should save us a lot of time if something happens. We don't need to have them just to use with Daddy, we can use them for anything. I think Pat can make a couple more scabbards. And you'll get used to plugging them in. Daddy has another doctor's appointment."

A few days later, the cook was in a foul mood at breakfast. I listened as he was telling Bud about Jacob while I drank my coffee.

"He just don't do things right," said the cook. "Look at that mess out back! He can't put things back where they belong! He can't even keep the gate to the garbage cans closed! We're going to have a bear problem around here before you know it! In fact, we already got one! Look!"

I got up from the table and went to the window. There was a black bear sow and two cubs making a mess out of the garbage by where the golf cart was parked.

"He's right," I said. "The culprits are out there right now."

Bud got up and hobbled over to the window. "We got a problem all right. If my brother wasn't the game warden, I'd shoot them right now! But I better call Fred and see what we can do. Honey, you open the door and holler at them—scare them off. But they've got a free meal, they'll be back!"

"Open the door an' holler at them," I said. "What do you want me to do, invite 'em in for breakfast?" I went to the door, opened it and hollered, "Here, in here! Breakfast is hot in here!"

At the sound of my voice, the bears ran off. "A load of buckshot in their behinds would help them move faster and help keep them away for good," said Bud, grinning. "Do you want to share your breakfast with them, Honey?"

"No," I answered. "But I didn't know what to say, so I thought I'd hone up on my social graces."

"Practice on people, not bears," said Bud. "Have Sally come in and talk to me."

"I'm already here," said Sally, pouring her coffee.

"We're going to have a bear problem here if we don't do something about it now," said Bud.

"I know. I was watching from the upstairs window," said Sally. "Don't you think Honey is improving in his social graces? I thought it was marvelous, inviting the bears in, although his tone of voice could have been more inviting."

Bud and I both laughed at Sally's comment. She came over, gave me a kiss, and sat down to drink her coffee.

Bud was still grinning as he watched the bears run away. "We'll need to inform the guests to keep a close eye on their kids. We don't want any intermingling with the bears. A mother bear can be pretty ferocious where her young are concerned. All of us will need to keep an eye out for them, everywhere. When you're out on the trail, your horses will let you know if you get close to one. Generally, the bears will leave before you get too close. And what ever you do, don't ever get between the sow and any one of her cubs! I'll call Fred, maybe he can bring a trap out here and relocate them. The farther away, the better, as far as I'm concerned. And the sooner the better!

"By the way, Cookie, that open gate might not be Jacob's fault. I might not have got the gate latched when I put the golf cart away last night, I can't remember. But don't be too rough on him, he may not have been at fault."

We finished our breakfast, informed the dudes of the bears and the possible dangers then went to the barn to saddle horses for the day's ride.

We spent the day moving cattle around into new pastures. I'm sure the dudes spent more time looking for bears than cows. With the bears showing up and having to do something about it, that was another problem that had to be dealt with. The summer was passing and although there was plenty of time left, we needed to stay on top of everything to make it run smoothly.

The following day, Fred and an assistant showed up with a big steel cage while we were gathering the saddle horses. As Sally, Pat, Richard, Jason, and I arrived in the kitchen for breakfast, Fred was positioning the cage.

The cage was a bear trap designed to capture bears or mountain lions alive without harming them. The idea was to capture the animals, then transport them to another isolated area and release them. I personally didn't think it would work, but didn't say anything. There were three bears to capture and only one trap.

We all went in for breakfast. Fred was explaining, "If we can get the sow in the trap, call me. I'll come up and tranquilize the cubs and then we can move them somewhere else."

I was glad I hadn't said anything about the plan not working. They already had things planned out and if I'd have said anything, I'd have disclosed my own ignorance.

For the next few days, everyone's interest was centered on the bear trap. It was the first thing they checked when they came in for breakfast and when they came to the lodge for any purpose.

Then early one morning, before sunrise, there was a big commotion down by the kitchen. It woke Sally up. I'm a sound sleeper and never heard anything. Sally woke me.

"What's happening? What time is it?" I wasn't fully awake yet.

"I think we've captured a bear," she said as she shook me. "Let's go look."

The cook was already in the kitchen when we got there. "Coffee will be ready shortly," he said, somewhat disgustedly.

"What's up?" I thought the cook was disgusted because he was up a little earlier than usual.

"We didn't catch anything worthwhile," he said. "Just a raccoon."

Sally was already outside looking at the trap. Bud had made his way out to the trap. He looked very disappointed.

"I'll have to call Fred and have him come out and remove the raccoon and then reset the trap. This bear is certainly causing us a lot of problems even though she hasn't showed up for a while."

Fred showed up later in the day, reset the trap, and took the raccoon. Before he left, he assured Bud that, "We'll catch her, sooner or later. The raccoon could actually cause you more problems than the bears, getting in the garbage and such."

A week passed without any activity around the bear trap. Some of the guests expressed regret that we didn't capture the bear before they left; they would have liked to have seen her. Newly arriving guests were advised of the possible encounter and we went about our regular ranch duties. The hired help still checked the bear trap regularly first thing in the morning, but the tourists were quickly losing interest. Some thought it was just a ruse.

Late one night, a commotion by the kitchen aroused Sally again. She woke me up. "We've got something in the trap," she said.

"Another raccoon?"

"I don't know, but I'm going to go see."

"Wait for me," I said. "I don't want you confronting a mad momma bear by yourself!"

We turned on the outside light and could see two bear cubs in the shadows.

"I think we've caught the sow," said Sally. "Now, how do we catch the cubs?"

"We'll let Fred worry about that," said Bud. He'd come

into the kitchen. "I'll call him first thing in the morning. He'll probably have to tranquilize them. What do you think they'll weigh?"

"I'll bet they don't weigh over a hundred pounds," I said. "They're still just babies. I think Fred needs to bring another cage for them cubs. I don't want to try an' put them in the same cage with their ma."

"Good idea, Honey," said Bud. "I'll let him know. We need to keep the guests away from this area so they don't run off the cubs in the morning. Sally, you better let the boys gather the saddle horses and you control the guests and keep them away from the bears. I maybe ought to call Fred tonight, the sooner he gets them out of here, the better off we'll be."

I know Sally was disappointed at not being able to gather the horses, but she realized the importance of leaving the bears alone, for the guests' safety and the bears' welfare.

"What time is it?" I was still tired.

"It's twelve thirty," said Sally.

"Well, it's too early an' too late for coffee. I'm goin' back to bed. It's already tomorrow."

"Good idea," said Bud.

"I'm following you, Honey. You're right," said Sally.

"Make a note of that, Bud! Sally says I'm right!"

The next morning while we were gathering horses, Fred arrived with another cage on a trailer. A veterinarian drove another truck. Fred had shot one of the cubs with the tranquilizer gun and the veterinarian had shot the other one. They had one of the cubs loaded into a cage and Pat and I loaded the other one. Those guests that were up were allowed to take pictures of the captured bears, but from only a distance.

"Where you goin' to turn 'em loose? I hope it's a long way from my folks' place," I said.

"We'll go about two hundred and fifty miles south and turn

them loose on the forest. They'll be all right and shouldn't return here."

Fred and the vet had breakfast with us and, after checking the recovery of the cubs from the tranquilizer, pulled out.

"That's one potential problem that's solved," said Bud. "I hope they don't come back. If they do, I'll have a special place for them on the floor. We could use a new bearskin rug!"

Just a Matter of Luck

A few days later, Missus Abercrombie and Bud returned from town with two more portable radios and chargers. Pat made scabbards for them so they could be tied onto the saddles with the front saddle strings. We took them everywhere we went on the ranch and tried them out. They seemed to work well, although in a couple of areas, they didn't work.

"Keep these areas in mind and remember the closest place they worked. If something happens we'll have to get to the best place to use 'em," I told everybody.

Quite often Sally would call me when we were separated out on the range and test out the radios. The cook was supposed to be monitoring the radios all the time and could tell where everyone was at almost any time. This became very embarrassing for me because every time Sally called me, she would end her call with, "I love you, Honey!"

This became embarrassing to me because the cook started ending his calls with "I love you, Honey!" as did Pat and Jason and Richard. I could feel my face becoming flushed every time I heard it. I knew everyone was just giving me a hard time, and I could take it, but it was embarrassing.

We went about our ranch duties, keeping the guests busy and tending to the cattle. We were busy enough that we hadn't given much thought to hiring another hand for extra help for the winter and I had figured that Sally, Pat, and myself could handle it.

One day, Pat came to me and said, "I think we need to check the broodmare bunch. I noticed some dust along that old road that runs through their range. That road isn't used much, except by the forest service or BLM. The dust I saw was made by an outfit movin' pretty fast—faster than what the government people would go if they were just out checkin' things."

I asked, "What do you think's goin' on?"

"I don't know," answered Pat. "But we ought to go an' check it out."

"I suppose Sally, Jason, an' Richard can handle things here," I said. "Think we ought to take the two-ton truck with horses? If we do, we can get out there quicker an' get back quicker."

"Good idea. We'll need a pair of binoculars, an' it might not be a bad idea to bring a radio."

The next morning Pat and I saddled our horses and let Sally and the other hands gather the saddle horses. We loaded our horses into the truck and I told Sally of our plans.

"Pat thinks we just need to check things out," I said. "I'm sure everything is all right."

Sally looked concerned. "We haven't had any problems out there in the past," she said. "I hope nothing's wrong."

"Pat convinced me that we need to check it out. Keep close to your radio, I'll be in touch."

Pat and I left and drove to the broodmare band's range. We rode mostly in silence, keeping a close eye out for the horses. Pat spotted the horses at the same time I did.

"There they are," he said.

"I see 'em."

Pat got out of the truck and climbed up on the cab with the binoculars. "Let's just see what's happenin' before we disturb 'em."

I couldn't get a good count on the horses but everything looked to be normal from this distance.

"What do you see through the glasses, Pat?"

I think we're missin' a colt, unless he's lyin' down. I can't really tell. Let's just watch 'em awhile."

"Looks like to me everything's normal. But," I said, spotting some dust, "they might be having some visitors, though. Look off to the west. That's too much dust to be caused by anything but a truck."

"That's a pickup truck with a horse in the back. I wonder what they're up to. It's not a government truck an' it's headed straight toward the broodmares. Unload my horse, Honey. I'll head down that way horseback. Give me some time, and then bring the truck. This might develop into an interestin' situation."

I backed the truck up to a bank and jumped Pat's horse out while Pat was still on the roof.

"You tryin' to slide me off this truck? I almost lost you," said Pat, as he climbed down off the top of the cab. "Just wait here until I give you a sign."

He handed the binoculars to me. "If you see anything strange, or my signal, come on the double!"

Pat tightened the cinch on his horse. "We might have someone tryin' to borrow a horse or two. You keep the radio in the truck."

I watched as Pat rode toward the horses, apparently unnoticed by the driver of the truck. The broodmare bunch started moving slowly toward the truck, probably thinking they were going to get fed.

The truck stopped, the driver got out and unloaded the horse. He got on and slowly rode toward the broodmares and I saw him take down his lariat rope. The stud came out to meet him and he quickly popped his rope across the stud's back. The stud turned away and the rider made for the mares, rope ready.

He hadn't noticed Pat, but Pat had been watching his every action. When the intruder headed toward the mares, Pat took down his rope and headed toward the rider, still unnoticed.

The rider selected a colt and made ready to rope him when Pat caught up to him and threw his rope. He caught the intruder and I thought he was going to drag him off his horse, like they did in the movies. But he didn't. He had the intruder caught on his horse and he wasn't giving him any slack.

When I saw that Pat had caught the guy, I started driving the truck toward them.

I couldn't hear what Pat was saying, but I imagined he was giving him a good cussing out.

When I got to them, Pat said, "What do you want to do with him? He's caught red handed tryin' to steal one of our colts."

I looked the intruder over carefully. "Hello George," I said.

The guy gave me a surprised look.

Pat also looked surprised. "You know this guy?"

"I just know who he is. He's not one of my friends," I said. "He was here last spring applying for the year-round job. He also stole my horse and donkey a couple of years ago while I was at the hospital after gettin' hurt at the rodeo. I don't know what we ought to do with him. He's kinda worthless. Just keep him under wraps, if he tries to start something, jerk him off that horse an' drag him awhile. I'll use the radio an' see who I can get a hold of. I think we need the sheriff's assistance."

I got Sally on the radio and told her to call the sheriff. I told her where we were and to have him come out—we'd caught a horse thief.

"Are you kidding? You can't be serious," she said.

"I'm dead serious an' if the sheriff ain't here pretty quick, there's goin' to be a dead horse thief out here. An' call me back, let me know when the sheriff will be here."

I saw Pat smile a little.

"All right," said Sally. "I'll call the sheriff. I love you, Honey."

About twenty minutes later, Sally called. "The sheriff should be there in about an hour. There's a patrol car in that part of the county, but it will take him awhile to get there over those back roads. I had to call the cook and have him call the sheriff, I'm out on a ride with some of our guests."

"We'll just sit here an' wait for him," I said.

"Okay, I love you, Honey."

"Me too, Darlin'." I turned the radio off.

"Pat, I think we ought to just sit here with George until the sheriff arrives. Keep him just like he is, the same way you caught him as evidence. If he tries anything at all, jerk him off that horse an' teach him a lesson. If you cripple him or kill him, it's okay with me."

"You talk pretty tough, little boy," said George.

With that comment, Pat backed his horse up, pulling George back, but not out of the saddle. "We don't need no comments from the peanut gallery," said Pat. "One more comment an' you'll be eatin' sagebrush an' dirt."

Pat sounded like he meant business and George didn't make any other comments.

"How many of these colts have you stole, George, an' where are they? There's a mare over there that looks like she's missin' her youngster," I said.

I didn't really see a nervous mare, but I was running a bluff. "You know all those colts are branded, don't you? It seems pretty stupid to me that you'd steal a branded colt. We saw you leavin' this area yesterday, goin' pretty fast. You can make it easier on yourself if you let us know now. The game's up."

George took the matter under consideration. "We got one down the road a few miles in that old set of corrals."

I got back on the phone to Sally. "Have Jason or Richard get in my truck an' come down here. There's one of our colts in the corrals a few miles from here. We'll need to haul him back to his mom."

Bud came on the radio. "I know right where those corrals are. I've been monitoring your call. I'll have Jason drive me out there."

"Better wait until the sheriff comes," I said. "George might have a partner an' the sheriff's got to come right by those corrals. We don't want to tip him off. Better call the sheriff an' have him check out the corrals before you show up."

"Good idea, Honey. Who's this George guy? Do you know him?"

"It's George Crawford, Bud," I said. "He's the guy that stole my horse an' donkey at the rodeo. I told you about it after we interviewed him about a job last spring."

"You keep him right there, Honey. I'll be there shortly and I'm bringing a gun. See you soon."

"I love you, Honey." It was Sally signing off.

"I love you too, Honey." It was Bud signing off.

"I love you too, Honey." It was the cook signing off. He'd been monitoring the radio transmissions.

"Me too," I said, laughing.

"It's gettin' hot out here," said George. "There's a couple of beers in my truck. Want one?"

"No," said Pat. "You just sit there. It's goin' to get a lot hotter for you."

George did some complaining, but as Pat tightened the rope, he quieted down.

After a spell, I could see George was getting tired. Pat looked like he was getting tired also.

"Want me to spell you, old partner?"

"Nope," said Pat. "I'm kinda enjoyin' this. 'Course we could end it right quick if Georgie here wants to try something."

"You holler if you want some relief," I said.

The deputy sheriff showed up and Bud and Jason were right behind him in my truck, with a spotted colt in the back. The deputy had a passenger in the back of his car.

"What do we have here?" said the deputy.

"That's just the way Pat caught him, tryin' to rope one of our colts. Pat's ready to give him a little sample of what it's like to be roped an' dragged some," I said.

"That won't be necessary," said the deputy. "He took a set of handcuffs from his car and handcuffed George while he was still on his horse. "You can join your partner in my car."

George got off his horse handcuffed and almost fell down.

I turned to Jason, who had driven my truck up to us and gotten out. Bud was still in the truck. He sat quietly, watching the situation.

"We'll want to press charges, deputy. Haul them in and put them in jail," Bud said.

"Before we do that, go find the broodmares an' unload that colt," I told Jason. "Stick around long enough to make sure the colt finds his ma, then you can go to town. Bud will be with you; he can tell if the colt mother's up. Don't leave until Bud says so."

Before Bud and Jason left, Bud said, "Honey, you stay here until we get back. I want you to go to town with me and fill me in on what happened. Jason can go back to the ranch with Pat."

They left in search of the mares. Pat had gotten off his horse, loosened the cinch, and loaded his horse in the two-ton truck.

"It got a little hot out there," he said, as he approached the deputy and me. "Too bad we didn't bring some water."

The deputy was filling out a preliminary report. "There's a canteen in the front seat of my car," he said. "Help yourself. Don't let the prisoners out!" He was grinning as he said that.

I answered questions as the deputy filled out his report.

Soon, Jason and Bud returned. "Honey, you and I are going to town to press charges. Pat and Jason can go back to the ranch."

I asked, "What do you want to do with George's horse and saddle?"

"There's another horse in the corrals back there. We'll take the horses back to the corrals and turn them both loose. They'll be all right. We'll leave the saddles there."

The deputy had overheard our conversation. "Better take both horses to your place and the saddles. We might need them for evidence."

"That makes sense," said Bud. "But I don't need you accusing me of horse stealing with his horses in my corral!"

The deputy laughed. "That won't happen and the county might even reimburse you for their feed. You guys can follow me into town. We'll get this deal done right directly."

We started out and only stopped at the corrals to load the other horse and pick up the other saddle. At the highway, we turned toward town following the deputy. Pat and Jason turned toward the ranch.

On the way, I told Bud what had happened. "Pat really did everything," I said. "I was just along for the ride. I hope Pat takes care of my horse, I forgot to ask him to."

"He will," said Bud. "He's a good hand, as you know. I suppose he'll let the cook know we'll be late for supper. We better get to a phone in town and tell the cook not to keep supper for us. We'll eat in town. I've got a feeling we'll be quite late getting home tonight.

"That was just a matter of luck that Pat noticed the dust yesterday," said Bud. "We were real fortunate. It's a good thing we didn't hire that George Crawford guy. Of course, if we would have, we might not be in this situation right now."

"Of course," I said, "If we had hired him, we might be in a worse situation!"

"You're probably right," laughed Bud.

In town, we filled out the necessary papers at the sheriff's office. "You'll probably need to come into town for the trial," said the deputy. "We'll notify you before that happens."

Bud and I left the sheriff's office and went to a café to get something to eat. I had to help Bud into the café. I called the ranch and told Sally not to keep supper for us. It had been a long day. We got back to the ranch well after dark.

The next day went on as usual, although I spent a lot of time telling the guests about the events of the previous day. I don't know what was more tiring—telling everyone about the previous day and answering questions or actually doing it.

We took the guests out for a scenic ride that day. We'd brand a few calves in a couple of days. We settled into our regular routine once again, but I found myself looking toward the broodmare range more often, just keeping my eyes open.

A few days later the sheriff came to the ranch. He had a summons for Bud, Pat, and I to appear in court the second day of August.

"You could have called with this," said Bud, as we all sat down to eat the noon meal. "You know we would have shown up."

"I suppose so," said the sheriff. "I know you would have shown up. But this is a legal document and it needs to be delivered in person."

I asked, "Where are the crooks now?"

"Suspects," said the sheriff. "They're suspects until proven guilty. However, the suspects are still in my jail. It seems …"

"That's a good place for 'em," I said, interrupting. "That's right where they belong."

"As I was saying," continued the sheriff, somewhat annoyed at my interruption, "we did a background check on both of them. There are outstanding warrants on both of them. It seems there's a 'failure to appear' warrant from a couple of years ago in conjunction with a drunk driving charge and a horse stealing charge. There are also some other charges, I don't remember exactly what they were. Were you involved in the horse stealing charge?"

"Yep," I said. "That was my horse an' donkey they stole. They were drunk when they did it an' I was with the sheriff when he took 'em to jail. How come they didn't stay in jail?"

"They were let out on bond," replied the sheriff. "They jumped bail an' never showed. I'm surprised they stayed so close rather than leaving the country completely. They're being held without bail now. The prosecuting attorney convinced the judge they were a flight risk. It didn't take much, they'd done it before.

"Well, guys, I've got to get going," said the sheriff, smiling. "We need to keep law and order in this county and that's my job. When you come for the trial, be prepared to spend a few days. They've been appointed the public defender, they don't have any money for a lawyer, and he's new to the job. He will probably try to make a name for himself. Thanks for dinner, it was real good!"

"These guys are being tried on charges of horse stealing. How do I recover my loss of time from them? I'd like to stick them with everything I can," said Bud.

"You better talk to your lawyer about that," said the sheriff. "It sounds like a civil matter to me."

"We'll see you in town, probably a day before the trial," said Bud.

Living in Town

The next couple of weeks went by without anything special happening. Guests left and arrived and we kept them busy if they wanted to stay busy. The weather stayed good, although some of the afternoons got hot.

However, one day the prosecuting attorney showed up and asked Bud, Pat, and I some questions about what happened. He seemed satisfied and left with the remark that, "This was an open and shut case. I don't foresee any problems."

The last day of July, Bud called Sally, Pat, Jason, Richard, and I into his office. "Pat, Honey, and I are going to town tomorrow for a few days to testify at that horse thief's trial. While we're gone, Sally will be in charge. You boys should pretty well know the routine by now, gather the saddle horses early each morning, find out who wants to ride, saddle their horses for them and take them out riding. Don't gather any cattle; we only have one more bunch to brand.

"There are some new guests arriving. Sally can pick horses for them. Handle everything just like it was your own place and everything will be all right. If you have some slack time, you can ride fence. Take the dudes … er … guests along. They can hold your horses while you make any repairs necessary. Any questions? Okay, you can go now. Sally, you stick around here for a minute."

"What do you need, Daddy?"

"I've made reservations for us at this hotel," said Bud, handing her a piece of paper. "You call me if you have anything you can't handle. I'll call you every night just to see how you're doing."

"We'll be all right," said Sally. "Don't you worry at all. This place will probably run smoother while you're gone than when you're here."

"That's what I'm afraid of," replied Bud.

After supper that night, I asked Sally, "Can you handle this by yourself while we're gone?"

"I think so," said Sally. "The cook or Missus Abercrombie can answer the phone, Jim and the maids can do their job. Jason, Richard, and I can handle the guests. It'll be a cinch. The hard part will be, well, you'll be gone."

"You'll get used to that," I said. "You might even come to like it!"

"Oh, I doubt that!" Sally was quite adamant about it.

"I better pack some clothes," I said. "I don't even have a suitcase. I don't know how long we'll be gone."

"You can use one of my suitcases," said Sally.

"Not the pink one!"

"No, silly, I'll help you pack. How many days do you think you'll be gone?"

"I don't know," I said. "Better pack for at least four."

The next day, Bud, Pat, and I went to town. I didn't know what to expect. Bud had made reservations at the hotel for us and we each had a private room.

"When you want to eat," said Bud, "just go down to the restaurant and order. Charge it to your room, I'll pick up the tab. If you want anything else, just call room service. While we're here, I expect to be treated as nice as we treat our dudes … er … guests."

"I suppose," said Pat, "we can live it up like the old days?"

"No! No! We don't want to do any damage," said Bud.

I suspected that Pat and Bud had lived some pretty wild days in the past.

"The trial is slated to begin at nine in the morning. We can actually walk to the courthouse from here. Well, I might not be able to. You can drive me and park the car. Just don't be late."

The next morning, we drove to the courthouse early, found a parking spot close and went to court. I was a little nervous and I guess it showed because Pat said, "Don't be nervous, Honey. You're not on trial. You ain't got anything to be nervous about, do you?"

"Certainly not," I said. "But I've never been to court before."

"Just be quiet and listen," said Bud, "you might learn something about our legal system."

The judge came in and we all arose. I wanted to ask why we did that, but Bud had said to be quiet.

The judge read the charges and asked the horse thieves how they pled. Their lawyer approached the bench and announced that the attorneys had reached a plea bargain.

The judge asked, "Just what did the councils agree to?"

"A reduced charge for a plea of guilty," replied the public defender. "The laws regarding horse stealing are outdated and antiquated. They shouldn't apply in this case."

"But there are charges for failure to appear with regard to another horse stealing charge."

"The defendant will plead guilty to this charge if the previous charge and failure to appear charge are dismissed."

"I have discussed this case with the prosecuting attorney," said the judge. "I have never been involved in a horse stealing case, and I'm curious. The court will take a thirty-minute recess. I would like to meet the councils and the victims in chambers."

The judge left the courtroom and the prosecuting attorney

and public defender and Bud, Pat, and I went into the judge's chambers. Inside the chambers, the judge took off his black robe, turned around and shook hands with Bud and Pat.

"How are you Howard?" Bud appeared to know the judge.

"Fine," said the judge. "And how are you Pat? This must be the young man referred to as Honey, correct? I've heard a lot about you."

"Yes sir," I answered, extending my hand to the judge.

"I'm fine Howie," said Pat. "How are you?"

"Fine, Pat, fine. You know Bud," said the judge, "I should disqualify myself from this case as I know you and Pat pretty well, and I probably will. But I'd like to hear the story first. Tell me what happened Pat."

Pat related the story about catching George Crawford while he was about to rope one of our colts.

The judge asked me, "What was your part in it, son?"

"I didn't do much, I was just kinda along for the ride. Pat did everything. I just called the ranch and had Sally call the sheriff. I didn't even unload my horse out of the truck."

"What was your involvement with the earlier incident?"

I explained how, two years earlier in another town about a hundred miles away, I'd entered the rodeo, got hurt and the sheriff took me to the doctor's. "When we returned," I said, "my horse and donkey were gone. The sheriff had put out a call on the radio and a highway patrolman answered it. He had the culprits outside of town and my animals were in their truck. One of the deputies drove me and my animals to the fairgrounds and that was it. I hadn't seen either one of them until the one feller, George, applied for a job with us last spring. We didn't hire him."

"Counselor for the defense," said the judge, "what is your client's part in this? Was this attempt at horse stealing a means to get even with the Wilson Ranch for not getting hired?"

"No, your Honor. The defendants both claim they had been drinking and didn't know what they were doing. They have both expressed a great deal of remorse over the incident."

The judge said, "I can imagine. Are you prepared to defend your clients in the original charge of stealing horses?"

"I haven't seen any of the original documents," answered the lawyer.

"Are you counselors prepared to accept my judgment in this case even though I know both these gentlemen? Are your clients?"

The attorneys nodded in agreement.

"I think," said the judge, "in the interest of time and judicial precedence, I shall disqualify myself from this case. I am very well acquainted with the victims and fully believe them, yet I haven't heard the defendant's side of the story. I think we can get this in Judge Reynolds court, perhaps as early as day after tomorrow. Counselors, make arrangements to get this in front of Judge Reynolds as soon as possible.

"Bud, where are you staying? Perhaps we can get together later and discuss old times. Of course, we'll have to bring Pat along just to keep us both honest."

"We're just down at the hotel," answered Bud. "Come by anytime."

They shook hands, the judge put on his robe and we returned to the courtroom. When the court proceedings resumed, the public defender asked for bail to be set for his defendants and the prosecutor objected saying, "They are both flight risks. They have jumped bail before and one of the charges is for failure to appear."

"Bail is denied," said the judge. "Next case."

Bud, Pat, and I left the courtroom. We got to the company car and drove to the hotel.

"What now?"

"Nothing to do now but wait," said Bud. "The prosecutor will let us know when we need to go back to court."

I asked Pat, "What are you goin' to do?"

"I dunno," answered Pat. "I'm not much used to bein' in town. What are you goin' to do?"

"I'm about in the same boat as you are. I might wander around town for a bit, just to look. I don't really have any ideas."

"I'd suggest you get a little rest and relaxation," said Bud. "We've got the busiest part of the summer ahead of us. I think I'll go to my room and rest. I'd suggest you do the same. I'll meet both of you for supper about six tonight."

Wandering around town didn't do much for me. I quickly got bored and returned to the hotel. I got something to eat and charged it to my room, as Bud had instructed. That was a strange feeling; I'd always paid for my purchases. I went to my room and tried to rest, but it didn't work. I was very restless. At the ranch, I could always find something to do and it generally was constructive.

At supper, we discussed the upcoming trial. The attorney had called Bud and told him the trial was set for nine o'clock the day after tomorrow. I was disappointed—I had another day of nothing to do.

I was up early the next morning and wasn't surprised to see Pat in the coffee shop early.

He asked as I sat down at his table, "You ready for another excitin' day in town?"

"An excitin' day of doin' nothin! I don't know how people do it."

"They all got jobs," said Pat. "That keeps 'em busy."

Bud showed up for breakfast. "Tomorrow we'll be in court. Make yourselves available, especially you Honey, in case the law-yer wants to go over our case with you. Honey, because those guys stole your animals earlier, you might be our star witness. Stick around in case you're needed."

"I've already seen all I need to see in this town. I've been bored ever since we left the courtroom yesterday," I said. "I don't know what to do today. I'll be glad when this is over."

"Me too," said Bud. "But it just comes with the territory. I just hope the bums get the book thrown at them. I detest thieves. Pat, how did you enjoy our visit with Howard last night?"

"It was good," said Pat. "Brought back a lot of old memories."

I asked, "How do you guys know the judge?"

"We go back a long ways," said Bud. "We used to bum around together."

I saw Pat smiling but knew I wasn't going to get more information out of them.

At nine o'clock the next morning, we were seated in court. When the judge came in I was surprised to see she was a woman. We all rose when she entered. The judge called the court to order. The charges were read and the defense attorney restated the plea bargain. The judge denied the plea bargain as she noted the defendants had previous horse stealing charges filed against them. Then she said something about a jury and the defendants had waived that option. I suppose in this country, composed mostly of cattle and horse people, their lawyer had advised them against a trial by jury; it would be difficult to get enough impartial jurors.

I settled back to listen.

Pat was called to testify and I listened closely. He told it exactly as it happened. The defense attorney only had a few questions for Pat regarding George Crawford's demeanor on the day we caught him. I thought the deal was over, as that was our case. However, I was called as the next witness. I was somewhat surprised to hear my given name. No one had called me that all year.

"Don't be nervous, Honey," said Bud, as I rose to take the stand.

I was sworn in and the prosecuting attorney asked me, "Are you the person commonly referred to as 'Honey'?"

"Yes sir," I answered.

The lawyer grinned. "How do you feel about that?"

"I can't get anybody to change it," I said.

That comment brought a laugh from the spectators in the courtroom. I saw Bud and Pat laugh and I could feel my face becoming flushed.

I was asked to recount the events of the day we captured George Crawford trying to rope one of our colts and I did. The defense attorney asked me pretty much the same questions he asked Pat and I answered them. Then I was asked to recount the events of the day two years previous when George Crawford had stolen Roman and Matilda, and I did. After I was done, I was dismissed from the stand.

The next witness was the sheriff from the town where I'd hurt myself at the rodeo. I hadn't seen him in court, but recognized him as soon as I saw him. He testified pretty much as I had, but he added some facts I wasn't aware of, particularly concerning the failure to show charge. I looked around the courtroom and recognized the highway patrolman that had pulled the two horse thieves over for drunk driving. I thought this might turn into a longer trial than I had expected or wanted.

The highway patrolman testified as to the events two years ago just as the sheriff. I made a mental note to meet both of them outside of court.

The defense attorney called some witnesses to the stand to testify as to George Crawford's and his accomplice's character. I wasn't impressed with any of the character witness' credibility; they looked more like his beer drinking buddies.

The judge called a short recess to confer with the attorneys and I went over and met the sheriff and highway patrolman from two years ago. It was good to see them.

"Looks like this George Crawford takes a particular liking to your animals," said the sheriff as we shook hands. "How are you?"

I filled him in on the events of the last few years and we visited with the highway patrolman for a while. Bud and Pat came over and as I started to introduce them, Bud already knew the sheriff although it had been some years since they'd met.

"You know Bud," said the sheriff, "this judge Reynolds is quite a horse lover."

"I'm not acquainted with her, but Howard informed me of that when we visited the other night. I feel pretty good about how this case is going, as they didn't offer up much of a defense."

"Well," said Pat, 'If you ask me they're ..."

Pat was interrupted by the bailiff. "Court is about to resume gentlemen."

We entered the courtroom and again rose as the judge entered the room. I could see rising for the lady judge, but why did we have to stand up for the man?

The judge called the court to order. She read off the charges and after each one she said, "Guilty."

Then she read off the sentences, the minimum and maximum for each charge, including the failure to appear charge.

Then she said, "This court finds you, George Crawford, guilty on all charges, sentences you to ten years in the state penitentiary on the first charge of horse stealing, ten years on the second charge of horse stealing and three years on the failure to appear charge."

Bud, Pat, and I all smiled. I saw the two sheriffs and highway patrolman smiling.

The judge read off George Crawford's accomplice's charges and he was sentenced to the same periods of time.

The trial was over. Bud contacted his lawyer and talked to him about recovering damages in a civil trial.

"I seriously doubt that it would be worthwhile," said the lawyer. "Where those two are going, they won't get much money and they haven't got any now."

"I guess twenty-three years is plenty," said Bud. "We won't have to worry about them for a while. We'll spend tomorrow in town; I'm taking you guys and Howard to supper. We'll go back to the ranch the next morning. If you need to do any shopping, you can do it tomorrow."

I was not particularly happy. I had another day in town and was already bored. I felt like another day would kill me, even though I was happy about the results of the trial.

Bud must have seen the look of disappointment on my face. "You might want to shop for something for Sally, Honey. I used to bring her a surprise every time I'd come back from town."

"I don't know of anything she really needs," I said.

"Get her something she don't need," said Pat. "Women are like that. They treasure stuff they don't need. They just like to have it around, an' look at it every now an' then."

"Got any suggestions?" I was at a loss.

"I'll go with you," said Pat. "Maybe I'll see somethin' that will work."

"You guys can figure that out tomorrow. Let's get something to eat and hit the sack. Tomorrow, we'll have supper with Howard at six. Don't be late. You'll be on foot, I need the car to take care of some business."

The next day, Pat and I ventured downtown, on foot. We must have walked into every store in town. I was starting to get tired. The only thing I thought Sally would appreciate was a big box of chocolates. I bought the biggest box I could find and decided to call it a day. I went back to the hotel and took a little nap before supper. Pat was still shopping when I left for the hotel.

At supper, I felt a little out of place, listening to the old timers hash out their bygone days. I was the youngest and while they occasionally tried to involve me in their discussion, I was content to sit and listen. Pat was the youngest of the three and Bud was the oldest. Howard, the judge, was somewhere in between them. I heard a lot of history that night, but soon tired. I excused myself and went to my room.

As I walked out the door, Bud said, "I haven't called Sally yet tonight. Honey, why don't you call her? Tell her how the trial went and let her know we'll be home tomorrow sometime after noon."

For the first time all day, I felt like I had something constructive to do. I called Sally.

"I miss you," she said when she heard my voice.

"And I miss you, too," I answered. I told her how the trial went and that we expected to be back to the ranch around noon.

"I'll have the cook keep something for you to eat," she said. "How are you holding up?"

"I've never been so bored for so long since I had my appendix out," I said. "I'm ready to come back to work. I forgot to ask you before I left, is there anythin' you need?"

"Just you here," she said.

"Well," I said, "I got you a little surprise. You probably don't want it, but will take it anyway, then tell me what a wonderful husband I am. But …"

Sally interrupted, "How did you know?" She was giggling.

"It was a just a wild guess," I answered. "But, as I was goin' to say, if you don't want 'em, I'll take 'em. How are things goin' there?"

"This place hasn't ever run so smooth," she answered.

"Are you sayin' we should leave more often?"

"No, no! I'm grateful things are going so well. But I don't really need anything. I'm sure your surprise will be enough. What are we going to do with these two horses we've got?"

I'd forgot about the George Crawford saddle horses. "I don't know," I said. "I'll mention it to Bud in the morning. We'll be home tomorrow an' maybe we can stir up somethin' excitin'."

After some more small talk, we hung up and I went to bed. I was ready to leave town and as far as I was concerned, the sooner the better.

The next morning, I packed my things and carried them along with Sally's surprise, down to breakfast.

"Looks like you're ready," said Pat.

"You bet!"

"We'll go as soon as Bud comes down and eats. It might be a little bit though, we were up pretty late last night."

"I'll be ready," I said.

Bud finally showed up, but not early enough for me. A bell-boy had brought his suitcase down.

"I forgot it yesterday," I said, "but what are we goin' to do with the horse thieves' horses?"

"The sheriff has contacted the Humane Society," said Bud. "They'll send someone out with a stock trailer and take them to town. I don't know what they'll do with them, probably keep them until someone, a relative perhaps, claims them. If nobody claims them, they'll probably be sold at the sale. We'll take a good look at their brands. If I know them, I'll call the brand owners and get their history. They might even be stolen."

As soon as Bud finished eating, he told Pat, "Bring the car around. I'll pay the bill and we'll get going. I hope you guys didn't break me with room service and the like!"

Pat took his bag and went for the car. I volunteered to carry Bud's bag. He would have had a tough time carrying his bag and supporting himself with two canes.

We were finally off. The farther we got from town and the closer to we got to the ranch, the better I felt. I started thinking of the things that would need to be done when we got home.

I generally can't sleep during the day, but I fell asleep on the way home in the backseat of the car. When I woke up, we were about five miles away from the ranch house and I had a stiff neck—I had fallen asleep in an awkward position.

"Another unexpected problem," I thought.

The Tough Get Tougher

Our arrival at the ranch caused some questions about the trial from Missus Abercrombie and the cook. We arrived after the guests had left on rides. Over the noon meal, which the cook had kept for us, Bud answered questions about the trial that seemed to be endless. Bud did enhance his story a little with each retelling, but it didn't differ much from what actually happened.

Sally, Jason, and Richard were out on rides with the guests. After eating, I went to the barn, walking gingerly, nursing my stiff neck. It was good to be home, even with the ailing neck. I slowly walked around the place, inspecting everything. Nothing was out of place. It looked like everyone had done a good job while we were gone.

I got some horse liniment and put it freely on my stiff neck. I always liked the smell of it and it seemed to help. Gingerly I moved my neck. It was painful but I would just have to turn my head frequently and work it off. I was hoping it would be gone by morning.

Jason and Richard returned with their riders. We took care of the horses and the riders went to the swimming pool. The swimming pool was a very popular spot after a ride for the guests.

"Where'd Sally go?" I was a little concerned that Sally was late.

"She took the longer ride," said Richard. "She told us she'd be in about an hour after we got back."

"That's just like her, to take the longest ride," I said. Secretly, I was proud of her and considered myself lucky to have caught her. Actually, she had caught me, but I still considered myself lucky.

About three in the afternoon, Sally called on the radio. "We're going to be a little late coming in," she told the cook. "We've had a horse come up lame. I've let the guest ride my horse and I'm walking, leading the lame horse."

The cook found me and told me what Sally had said. "Where are they?"

The cook told me where Sally and her riders were. I saddled my horse, Roman, and another horse for the guest to ride and went out to meet them.

Pat saw me leaving and asked, "Need some help?"

"Nope," I answered. "This should be pretty simple, one of the horses just came up lame."

I left leading the extra horse in the direction Sally would be coming from. I found them about five miles from the ranch. Sally was leading the horse that was limping painfully. She looked relieved to see me, but still concerned about the horse.

"I thought you might need a ride," I said, giving the lead rope to Sally.

"That was kind of you," she said.

"What's the problem?"

"I'm not sure," she said. "I don't know if it's a ligament, a tendon, or just a stone bruise."

I got off my horse to look at the lame horse. Sally immediately gave me a big kiss, much to the amazement of the guests.

"It's all right," she explained to the guests, "he's my husband. You smell like you brought the horse liniment!"

The guests laughed.

"I've got a stiff neck," I said, although I had almost forgotten about it.

I looked over the lame horse while Sally put the guest on the extra horse I'd brought and adjusted the stirrups.

"I don't know if it's a ligament or tendon," I said. "I halfway suspect it's a ligament. You folks can go on ahead an' I'll lead the horse in. If you don't get movin', you'll be late for supper."

Sally waved and winked at me and left with the guests. I started out, leading the lame horse. "Some liniment will help whether it's a ligament or tendon," I thought to myself.

I soon lost sight of Sally and her riders, but proceeded slowly toward the ranch. After a while, I saw a rider approaching me. It was Sally.

"I brought you a bottle of horse liniment," she said. "I also thought you might want some company."

"That's nice of you," I said. "But I put plenty of liniment on my neck earlier an' it's startin' to feel better."

"It's not for you, silly, it's for the horse!"

"Oh! You care more for the horse than you do for me!"

"No. You can have some after you use it on the horse."

I got off Roman and went to get the liniment from Sally. As she handed it down to me, she leaned down and gave me another kiss. My neck was still a little painful and I backed away.

Sally looked surprised. "Maybe you ought to use some more of that on your neck."

"It'll be all right. It's already startin' to feel better," I said, as I applied the liniment freely to the horse. The excess on my hands I wiped onto my neck. I got back on my horse and we started home.

"You're goin' to be late for supper," I said.

"So are you. Tell me about the trial."

I related the story of the trial and its outcome on the way

back to the ranch. Sally didn't have any questions about it and I was glad. I'd had enough of town and the trial.

"How did things go here?"

"Things went well while you were gone," said Sally. "This lame horse is the only problem we've had. We had some folks leave and some more showed up."

"It doesn't sound like things went well," I said. "We leave for a few days an' you let one of our best horses come up lame!"

I was teasing Sally and she knew it. But she wasn't going to let me have my fun with her.

We got back to the ranch and took care of our horses. I put more liniment on the lame horse then wrapped the lower leg with an Ace wrap bandage doused in liniment.

After supper, I gave Sally her box of chocolates.

"That's just what I wanted! You are truly the best husband ever! Do you want one?"

I wasn't surprised by Sally's reaction. She'd said pretty much what I thought she would.

Later that night, after everyone had turned in, I heard a commotion in the hallway. I checked and found Bud, lying in the hallway.

"What happened?"

"I fell," said Bud. "I'm getting to the point where I can't support myself with these two canes."

Sally came out. "Are you all right, Daddy?" She came to his side where I was helping him up.

"I'm okay daughter."

I steadied Bud while Sally got his canes. We both helped him into his room. "That pair of crutches I used when I broke my foot is out in the storage shed. If you'll be kind enough to get them, I'll start using them tomorrow. I've got to be able to get around!"

I got the crutches from the shed and took them to Bud's room.

"Thanks Honey. I'll be able to get around some now."

I went to Sally's and my living quarters.

"I'm really concerned about Daddy," said Sally. "He seems to be getting worse rather than better. I don't know what to do."

"I don't think there's anything we can do," I said. "Bud will do whatever he can. He's a fighter."

"I know. But I feel so helpless!"

The next day, Bud came to breakfast on the crutches. He appeared to be in good spirits, but I wondered if this was just an act.

The next few days were uneventful and we seemed to be settling into the normal routine. Bud would come down to the barn in the golf cart occasionally, but it was difficult for him to get around on foot. He was always available to visit with the guests and he spent a lot of time with Matilda and Einstein and the kids.

The Humane Society sent a woman out with a stock trailer to get George Crawford's horses. Jason and I came out to meet her.

"What can you tell me about these horses?" The woman seemed kinda bossy and more impressed with her position than we were. "They look like they've been abused in the past!"

"They ain't been abused while they been here," I said. "The horses belong to a convicted horse thief named George Crawford who is currently doin' time in the state pen. We captured this ..."

"The state penitentiary! My goodness! And he stole horses?"

"Yes ma'am," I said. I thought I'd have a little fun with the woman. "Pat an' me was just about to lynch him when the sheriff showed up an' stopped us. He's a pretty bad character. But, it's a good thing the sheriff showed up, or we might be in jail ourselves.

"Jason, get Richard an' bring those saddles down here."

"But I'm just supposed to pick up these horses," said the woman.

"The saddles go with them," I said.

When the boys showed up with the saddles, I had Jason and Richard saddle each horse. "That's the way they come to us an' that's how they're leavin'."

We loaded the horses in the trailer.

"The sheriff will know what to do with the saddles," I said.

"What will happen to the horses? I'd like to own one," the woman said.

"If no one claims them, they'll probably be sold at auction. You could probably buy one there," I said. "Now you drive careful!" I wanted the woman to leave.

"Oh, here," she said as she handed me an envelope. "I'm supposed to give this to you."

"Thank you. Now you drive extra careful. You have two animals behind you."

The woman drove slowly out of the yard. I put the envelope in my pocket and promptly forgot about it.

The tourist season was fast coming to an end. School would start after Labor Day, and then our tourist season would essentially be over. We would have a few guests that didn't have school-age children, and we could take longer rides if the guests wanted to.

During a lull one day, I cornered Bud and asked him, "How do you feel about the way this past summer went?"

"It's been a good summer," replied Bud. "We had the wedding, we captured a couple of horse thieves, we captured some bears and relocated them, and we didn't get anybody hurt; it's been a good year."

"I mean business-wise," I said.

"Oh," said Bud. "Financially, we're better off this year at this time than we were last year. We've got a lot of the same people coming back next year. If we can get a good price for our calves we should turn a tidy profit. Why do you ask?"

"I noticed that some of our cows are starting to show some age. We might want to cull a little heavier this year an' hold back more replacement heifers. Pat had said something about you not keeping any replacements."

"I had toyed with that idea, but I think we'll probably do just as you've said."

"Are you goin' to take in any hunters this year?"

"No," said Bud. "I'd prefer not to anyway. Of course if you or Pat wants to hunt, you certainly can. We could certainly use the meat."

"I think we ought to post the ranch, NO HUNTING. Hopefully that will keep the hunters away," I said. I didn't much care for the hunting season.

"We'll post it, HUNTING BY WRITTEN PERMISSION ONLY. That way Pat and you can hunt. And if anybody else wants to hunt, we'll give them permission, for a fee."

"What'll you charge?"

"I don't know," said Bud. "Whatever comes to mind, I guess. Maybe I ought to call Fred and get some ideas."

"The next time someone goes to town, have them pick up some signs and we'll take the dudes around the ranch and post them," I said. "That will give use something worthwhile to do while we're ridin' around. Oh, by the way, the woman from the Humane Society gave this to me. I forgot all about it."

I handed Bud the envelope and he opened it.

"It's a check for the feed for those two horses. We'll get you the signs."

Labor Day came and, other than a few childless couples, we were essentially out of the dude business for the year. The maids packed their things and Sally drove them to town. Before they left, Sally told them they could have their jobs next year if they wanted to come back.

Jason and Richard gathered up their belongings and I took them to town the next day. I also told them that we'd be pleased to have them back next year.

All of the help that was left at the ranch was Bud, Sally, Missus Abercrombie, Pat, the cook, and I. The cook's helper had left a week earlier and Missus Abercrombie had been helping out in the kitchen. We did have four couples, three older couples and a pair of newlyweds. It was strange not to have a lot of people around, but I thought it was nice.

The older folks were content to go on hour or hour an a half rides and Sally would take them. The newlyweds were more adventuresome and wanted to ride longer. Pat or I took them on the longer rides checking the cattle.

On these longer rides Pat and I would generally discuss the affairs of the ranch. Fall was approaching and we'd need to gather the cattle, sort off the calves, and do some culling from the cow herd. We'd need to select some replacement heifers. We'd also need to run in the broodmare bunch and wean the colts. We'd halter break the colts during the winter. We'd also need to go to some bull sales during the winter and get some replacement bulls.

I was a little concerned. Even with Sally helping, we could use an extra man as Bud wasn't any help at all in his condition. If we didn't get extra help it would mean a lot of riding and take a lot of time. We could manage, but it would be difficult.

"Has anybody come around lookin' for a job?" Pat asked, obviously thinking the same thing I was.

"Bud hasn't said anything," I said. "We might have to get him to put an ad in the paper or list with an employment agency. But, I'd rather do it alone than with the wrong person."

"Me too," said Pat.

"And if we're going to breed the replacement heifers artificially next spring, we'll need some extra help then."

"I don't know what Bud's plans are," said Pat, "but it looks like you're on top of things."

"We'd better do something while we're on top of things before we get so far behind we can't get caught up. Do you know anybody that might be lookin' for work an' would fit in?"

"Not off hand," said Pat. "I'll give it some thought an' let you know."

"How 'bout some people that have worked here in the past?"

"In the past it's been mostly college kids," said Pat. "They've generally only worked one summer. Bud should have a bunch of their applications on file. Maybe you could look through them."

"I'll give it a shot," I said.

Later, I mentioned our hired help situation to Sally. "Do you have any applications from former employees that we might consider hiring? If you do, we'll go through them together and see if we can contact them about working for us."

"I'll see what we have," she said. "Daddy doesn't generally keep them very long."

"We can also write up a help wanted ad an' put it in the feed stores an' saddle shops next time someone goes to town. We might want to put somethin' in the help wanted column in the paper."

"I'll get on it," said Sally.

A few days later, Bud asked me, "What are your plans for the winter?"

"I'm stayin here, of course," I replied. "I figured on doin' everythin' just like you've done it in the past."

"No! I don't mean that," said Bud. "What are you going to do to replace me? You know I can't do much."

"Who have you been talkin' to?"

"Sally has mentioned something. But what are you going to do?"

"The way I got it figured, we need to hire another man an' we need to hire him soon enough to help with the fall gather. We also need to get a tub grinder."

"I can see the hired man, but why the tub grinder?"

"We need the tub grinder so we can increase the nutrition level in our replacement heifers. They won't cycle unless all their other needs are met. We can mix some grain and pour it out of the grinder into the feed bunk. We're goin' to breed the replacements here, so we want as many to start cyclin' as possible."

Bud asked, "Are you sure you know what you're doing, Honey?"

"Yep. I been doin' some studying an' even that old advertisement that convinced you to send the heifers to the feedlot stresses the importance of a higher level of nutrition to get these heifers to breed as yearlings."

"If you say so, Honey," said Bud. "Who do you want to hire?"

"I haven't talked to anybody yet," I said. "You got any suggestions?"

"I do know one guy that's highly qualified, but he may not be available," said Bud.

"Who's that?"

"He's a feller that goes by the name George Crawford," said Bud, grinning.

"Never," I said. "Not even in twenty-three years!" I could see Bud was having some fun with me. "We don't need his kind around here!"

"I'll put an ad in the paper and have some ads printed up to put in the various stores," said Bud.

"Do we need to have 'em printed?"

"I think so," replied Bud. "If we have a printed ad, we're liable to attract some higher class people. Of course we'll get a lot of the run-of-the-mill kind, but if we're going to hire someone year round, we want a pretty special person. He has to be able to do it all, dudes, cattle and horses."

Bud got up on his crutches and started to leave. "I'm going to have hand controls put on the company car, I'll have Missus Abercrombie drive me to town tomorrow and get the ads printed up."

Bud left and I wondered just how long he could keep going. He'd went from a cane to two canes to crutches in what seemed like to me a very short time. He'd given up his horseback riding for a golf cart. And now hand controls on the car. I wondered what would be next.

When Bud returned from town, he'd had hand controls installed on the car. He also had another set. "We'll put them on the golf cart," he said. "I'll be darned if I'm going to be kept in the lodge!"

Gathering Cattle

Toward the end of September, we started getting a few calls regarding our help wanted ad. We were only willing to interview those people that could come out to the ranch. None of us wanted to go to town and spend a few days. A few applicants were somewhat disappointed; they didn't have transportation to the ranch.

To those people that didn't have transportation and expressed some sorrow that they couldn't come to the ranch, Bud would tell them, "Get a horse! That's how we hired our foreman; he came riding in and we kept him!"

A few of the people that came out, we didn't hire for what seemed like to me obvious reasons. One fellow had a good deal of empty beer cans in the back of his pickup. I didn't want anybody that drank and neither did Bud. Our experience with the hunter the previous fall had convinced me that we didn't need any drinkers on the place. We didn't hire anybody that needed a shave or didn't show up in clean clothes. Bud was kinda particular with regards to his hired help, and I was surprised that I had been allowed to stay on when I showed up, covered with trail dust as I was.

After considering a number of applicants with a good deal of cowboy experience, we tried to sort through the applicants to find out who would work out with the dude aspect of our business in the summer. Quite often, the older applicants would have the necessary experience with cattle and horses, but we felt they might have a tough time getting along with the dudes. A certain degree of diplomacy was required in the dude business.

After a good deal of discussion between Bud, Sally, Pat, and I, we finally settled on a feller named Dwight Davidson. He had some cattle experience and had done some guiding for hunting camps. He had never been around a dude ranch before. He was a few years older than I was, but apparently outgoing and friendly.

I thought his demeanor, having been around hunting camps before, might be a little harsh on a dude ranch and Bud expressed the same concerns, but we hired him on a trial basis. We wouldn't be able to tell just how he would get along with the dudes until the following spring and summer, but he was told he'd be on a trial basis for a year. He accepted the deal.

Pat said, "He seems like a nice enough guy. I'll take him aside and kinda instruct him as to how we handle our guests during the winter. He should be all right."

Dwight moved his stuff into the bunkhouse and went right to work the next day. He had his own saddle and equipment and we assigned him a horse. Pat, Sally, and I took him out to show him a little of the ranch. It also gave us an opportunity to see how well he could ride.

He could ride well enough, and we explained the operation of the cattle aspect of the ranch. He had a few questions that were applicable for the situation, and I thought he would work out okay.

A few days later, Sally, Pat, Dwight, and I saddled up early and started to gather cattle. Missus Abercrombie stayed with Bud, saying "I'm not really up to longer rides anymore."

It had started to get colder and we'd had a few snow flurries, but the snow didn't stick. It was a good time of year—cool, crisp mornings, warming up nicely in the afternoons.

Our first day gathering cattle went well; we found a lot of cows and calves. Bud and Miss Abercrombie were at the corrals when we corralled the cattle, and they were careful to stay out of sight with the golf cart until we had all the cattle in the corral. The next day should be fairly easy. After that the gather would be harder, with longer rides and fewer cattle each day.

I had gotten a count on the cattle when we corralled them and told Bud what the count was.

"Not quite half of them," he said. "The calves look good, don't they?"

"Yes," I said. "They've done well. We'll see just how good they are when we get the rest of them an' sort them off. Even the Longhorn crosses have done better than I thought they would. They've got a lot of size, but not as much flesh as the others. Maybe the cattle buyers will like that. There's a lot of color there."

"I hope the buyers like that," said Bud. "Right now this idea of breeding the replacements to calve as two year olds seems to be going good. We won't really know until we preg check in a few days. It'll be interesting to see how many of them heifers have rebred. We'll be able to tell how many replacements we'll need this fall."

We separated the bulls, cows, and calves and turned the cows out into a holding pasture. We'd run them in and pregnancy check in a few days after we did whatever we could to find the missing cattle.

We put the calves into a feedlot pen and fed them. We were teaching them what a feed bunk is. The cattle buyers liked that. After we preg checked the cows, we would separate the steers from the heifers and then select our replacement heifers. We would need to separate the Longhorn crosses from the others. Our weaning process had begun.

The next day we gathered again, with about the same

amount of success we had the day before. I got another count on the cattle we'd gathered and told Bud.

"We're short about twenty-five head again. It'll take some riding to bring in the stragglers. It seems like we come up short every year."

"You don't think they've been stolen, do you?" I asked. The events of the previous summer with the broodmare bunch and George Crawford were still vivid in my mind.

"I don't think so," said Bud. "We always have a few cows stray off the range every year. I'll give the neighbors a call and see if they've found any of our cattle. We haven't got any of theirs this year. We'll have to do some more riding the next couple of days and see what we can get before we preg check. I'll call the vet and see when he can come out. He'll need a couple of days to do the job."

We sorted off the calves from the cows and turned the cows into the holding pasture along with the cows we'd gathered the day before.

Dwight seemed to be holding up well, it appeared like he'd done a lot of riding in the past.

The next day we saddled up fresh horses to gather again.

Pat said, "Why don't we load the horses in the two-ton truck and drive to the far end of the range? We can save some time an' come back tomorrow for the truck."

"Good idea," I said. "Why didn't I think of that?"

We loaded our horses in the truck and drove to the far end of the ranch. We split up to cover more ground. Before we left, I told Dwight, "You push anything you find straight north an' you'll be headed toward the ranch. We'll meet at the gate on the south end where we came through the last two days. Bring everything you find, even if it's the neighbor's." I gave him fairly detailed instructions as I didn't want him to get lost.

We rode hard that day. Sally and I rode together for a while then split up. We'd found a few cows and I had Sally take them toward the ranch while I made a larger circle. I didn't find any more cattle, but Sally had found a few more. Pat and Dwight had found some cattle and when we met, I counted them and it looked like we had all our missing cows and a few extra.

"We've got some of the neighbor's cows," I said. "We'll take 'em in an' Bud can call an' have the neighbor's come an' get their cows."

Pat said, "Why don't you take the cattle in an' I'll go back an' drive the truck in? It'll save us some time tomorrow, an' I can probably make it back to the ranch before you get there. You don't have enough cows where you need me anyway. I'll put some hay out in the big corral to feed these cows tonight an' have the cook keep supper for you."

"That's a good idea, Pat. I'm glad to see that you're not only concerned with our cattle's welfare, but also ours." I was kidding Pat a little. "Do you want to go with him, Sally?"

"No," she said. "I'm here for the duration."

Sally never quit until the whole job was done.

"How you holdin' up Dwight?" He looked like he was a little tired.

"I'm okay." Although he was tired, he wasn't going to quit, especially when Sally was not leaving.

Sally asked, "What about you, Honey?"

"Don't bother about me," I said. "I feel like I'm just gettin' started."

Pat started to leave, but before he left, he said, "We'll see how you feel when you get to the ranch. It'll be after dark." He was grinning when he left.

We started the small cow herd toward the home ranch and didn't have any problems on the way. We got to the ranch after dark. The corral gate was open and Pat had put hay out. All we had to do was close the gate, take care of our horses, eat, and take care of ourselves.

When we went into supper, Bud said, "I've already called the neighbors. They'll send a man tomorrow to get their cows. He'll be here about noon. We'll sort off their cows and calves, and then sort our cows and calves. The vet will be here in two days to preg check. It'll take him a couple of days and I told him we'd put him up here and feed him. He's bringing an assistant to spell him when he gets tired. We should be able to get through the cows pretty quick.

"We'll sort off the open cows so we can sell them. I've called some cattle buyers; they'll be here next week. We'll sort the steers from the heifers then sort off what heifers we want for replacements. At the same time, we can sort off the Longhorn crosses. Let's remember to put the Holsteins we grafted onto those heifers that lost their calves with the Longhorns. That heifer we put with Matilda and Einstein needs to go with the open cows; she didn't have a chance to breed this year. When the calves and open cows are gone, we'll pretty well have it done for the year."

I asked, "What about the bulls?"

"I'd almost forgot them. We'll sort off the old bulls and have them ready for the buyers. Honey, when the buyers go into the corrals, you and Pat go with them. You can let me know what kind of offers they make you and we'll all make a decision."

"Sounds good to me," I said. I'd been a little concerned about selling the calves without some assistance, as I'd never done it before and wasn't really familiar with what the prices were and what the "shrink" would be.

When the vet showed up, we went right to preg checking the cows. I ran the squeeze chute, Pat kept the chutes full, and Dwight ran the gate that the open cows went into. Sally hurried the cows down the alley to the proper pen. She was the only one horseback. The vets alternated checking the cows and they would mark the open cows. I would call out to Dwight "open," and he'd swing the gate to put the cow in the pen. The open cows were going to be sold. The cows on this outfit had to produce a calf every year to pay their way, or they'd be gone.

Bud was present at the chutes, on his crutches. He couldn't do anything, but he was there, and he looked over every cow critically. Occasionally, he'd have a cow with a lot of age cut into a separate pen. "We'll keep these cows in during the winter and give them a little extra help. We might sell them as pairs after they calve. That would be better than having them die out on the range and leppy their calf," he said.

In two days, we had the herd checked. I was a little disappointed, about fifteen percent of the first calf heifers didn't rebreed. Bud noticed my concern.

"Don't worry about it, Honey. I'm told that's about par for the course. You need to remember, we've got about eighty-five percent more calves to sell this year than we've had in the past."

"Are you sure the math's right? It doesn't compute to me," I said.

"I'll do the math later. We've still got more calves to sell this year and I like that. We even have a few more cows to sell, and I like that. The last time I looked, prices were up a little from last year. I'm feeling pretty good about it. I'm even thinking we might need to keep a few more heifers back for replacements."

"Don't forget to get that tub grinder," I said. "If we can raise the nutrition level, I'm sure the replacements will rebreed at a higher percentage." I was concerned about the cattle aspect of the operation.

The next day, Pat and I sorted off the heifers we wanted for replacements. We took more heifers than we needed, knowing that all the replacements would not rebreed after they calved in two years. Bud didn't come into the corrals or alley, but he carefully scrutinized each heifer we cut into the replacement pen. It was a fairly simple operation; we took the biggest heifers as long as their conformation was structurally correct. As we'd pass on some of the heifers, Bud would question our choice.

Either Pat or I would say, "To small!" Bud didn't question our decisions.

When we had finished our sorting, I asked Bud, "What do you think of our decisions?"

"I would have taken a few of the heifers you cut off, they're good heifers."

"They were a little smaller than we wanted," said Pat. "But I think overall we've got a good bunch of heifers. We can take a few more if you want, but we've got more than we originally planned on."

"If you and Honey think that's good, then it's good with me. What do you think, Sally?"

"I think my husband and Pat have done an excellent job! Look at those heifers. They'd look good in anyone's herd."

I was surprised at the reference to "my husband." I was wondering if Sally was joking or really impressed and wanting to impress Bud.

"If you're satisfied, then I am too." Bud was slowly giving up management of the ranch.

After the noon meal, Pat, Dwight, and I saddled our horses and Sally got a fresh horse. We went to the bull pasture. We gathered the bull pasture and brought everything in.

"Why do we need to bring in everything? It seems to me we could just bring in the old bulls," said Dwight.

"We'll want to take a good look at everything," I said. "We might find a few younger bulls that haven't grown as we expected them to. Make sure you give the bulls plenty of room, if they get to fightin' they don't much care what they run into, especially the one that loses. Sally, we don't want you doin' a repeat of what you did with the bull a while back."

Dwight asked, "What did she do?"

I explained how a bull had tipped Sally and her grulla horse over a while back. "See that scar on the horse's flank? That's a reminder of the incident."

Dwight carefully eyed the grulla's flank. "Was anybody hurt?"

"Sally had to be taken to the doc's," I said.

"Totally uncalled for," said Sally.

"But necessary," I corrected.

We put the bulls in the corral and Pat brought them, one by one, down the alley. We looked over each bull carefully. The old bulls were put in the cull pen along with a younger bull or two that Pat or myself didn't care for.

Bud had come down in the golf cart to look over our culls. He thought we were right with the old bulls, but questioned our choices on the younger bulls.

He asked, "What's wrong with them?"

"That bull is pretty weak in the hindquarters," I answered. "So is the other one. They're built more like race horses than bulls. We need to get bulls that will pass on muscle, that's what we're sellin', and eventually meat."

Bud didn't argue. "We'll see how well you select bulls this winter!"

Pat just laughed.

The cattle buyers showed up a few days later and looked into each pen, without going in. We'd moved the replacement heifers away, as we didn't want the buyers trying to buy what was to become our cow herd.

Bud had Sally show the buyers to their rooms. He knew most of them, he'd done business with them before. Part of the deal was to provide a room and meals for the buyers. Bud felt that this put the buyers in a better mood and he could command better prices.

"Besides that," he'd say, "we have the accommodations. Why not use them to the benefit of the ranch?"

I did hear one of the buyers say, "Even if I don't buy any cattle, the rooms and food are well worth the time!"

The next day, everyone went to the corrals. I entered each corral with one buyer, listened to his offer and reported to Bud. We ended up selling the heifers to the buyer who said he'd take them all with no "shrink."

Bud explained to me that, "Shrink is a percentage that's taken off the weight after the calves are weighed. It's meant to compensate the buyer, but it really hurts the seller. The calves have already shrunk while they were on the truck."

We had separated the steers into two different groups, the larger steers and the smaller ones. A few of the buyers made offers on the steers, wanting to cut back a percentage of the smaller steers of each group. Bud wouldn't go for it, and he ended up selling the bigger steers to one buyer and the smaller steers to another.

By this time it was noon and everyone went to the lodge for a simple meal of cold cuts.

"We'll make the noon meal real simple and cheap," Bud explained to me. "I don't want to feed those guys that didn't buy anything. Sometimes I think some of them just come out for a free meal, as ridiculous as they're offers were. You've done a good job so far, Honey."

When we took the buyers into the Longhorn cross pens, we had some fun. Bud explained that, "These calves are out of our first cross heifers, they're all Longhorn crosses. They might make some good prospects for a roping club. Some of these calves can really run. We had a time getting them in. You guys can look them over, the steers are over here and the heifers are over there."

One of the buyers asked, "Don't you want to keep some of the heifers for replacements? There's a lot of color there; they might fit in with your horse herd pretty nicely!"

Bud just laughed. "You can ride any of them you want to!"

Offers were made on the Longhorns and while they didn't bring as much as the other calves, I thought they brought a pretty good price. When the Longhorns were sold, we moved to the cull cow pen.

Some of the buyers were not interested in the calves, just the cows and bulls. These buyers were interested in purchasing for a packing plant where the animals would be slaughtered and the carcasses made into hamburger. These buyers were making some fairly high offers for our cull animals and I thought the demand for hamburger must be fairly high.

Bud accepted a fairly high offer on the cows and we moved to the bull pen. The demand for the bulls was even better than for the cows and Bud accepted the highest offer.

"These cattle you have bought are going to be kept in the same pens they're in now until you have your trucks show up," said Bud. "You can stay here until your trucks move out with the cattle. We'll help you load them. You can use our phone to call for your trucks. Supper will be at six."

The buyers that didn't buy anything left and the successful buyers sat around in the lodge visiting. They all knew each other and it was interesting to listen to them visit. A semi tractor and trailer showed up around five.

"That's my truck," said the buyer that had bought the bulls. "Let's go get them loaded."

Pat, Dwight, and myself got up. "We can do this," I told the other buyers and Sally, who had also got up. "It won't take long."

We got the bulls loaded and invited the driver in for supper.

"Nope," said the driver. "I've got a ways to go. These bulls are to be at the packing plant in the morning."

"Make sure you get a weight on them before they're slaughtered," I said. "They will weigh up pretty good."

The driver left and the three of us went to get cleaned up for supper.

Trucks started arriving before daylight the next morning. We loaded each truck with the proper cattle, bringing up the number of animals the driver wanted for each compartment. We spent all day shipping the cattle out and I knew I'd put in a day's work when we were done. By nightfall, we had all the cattle loaded and shipped. I was pleased with Dwight's work. He had been around cattle before and knew what he was doing.

Our cattle sale had been a success, according to Bud. "We got the right prices," he said. "The calves just have to weigh up. I think we did real good on the Longhorns. They weren't carrying much flesh, but they were large-framed. I think they might surprise the buyer with their weight. I'm sorta tickled about that! The demand for the bulls was good."

"They'll be slaughtered this morning according to the driver," I said. "Somebody must have a pretty big order for hamburger. I invited the driver in for supper last night, but he said he had to hustle to get the bulls to the packin' plant on time. I reminded him to get a weight on them."

"Good," said Bud. "We'll do all right on them. We might even make enough to replace them. That would be a good trade, trading old bulls for breeding-age bulls."

"What bull sales do you want to go to?" I asked.

"We'll figure that out in November," said Bud. "Now, I want you to take these forms and carry a few of them with you while you're riding."

Another Hunting Season

"What are these forms?"

"These are forms with the names, addresses, and phone numbers of the hunters we'll let hunt on the property. We'll charge them twenty-five dollars to hunt for the season. Get it in cash. Also get their license plate numbers, I forgot to have them put on the form. Find out where they're camped. If someone doesn't want to pay, don't argue with them. Get as much information as you can, call me on the phone and I'll get a hold of Fred. We'll do what we can, but leave it in his hands."

Pat asked, "Are you sure you don't want us to throw 'em off the property? That might be more fun!"

"True," said Bud, "but remember they've got loaded guns. We'll do best to let Fred handle it legally."

"That ain't the way we used to do it," said Pat. He was grinning as he said that and again I got the idea that both Bud and Pat had some pretty wild days when they were younger.

The next day we ran in the broodmare bunch. Sally and I led them in and Pat and Dwight followed. I noticed Pat had replaced his lariat rope with his bull whip, but he didn't have to use it. We separated the mares from the colts. We would start halter breaking them in a few days.

The only chores we had were to feed the replacement heifers, feed the weaner colts, and run in the saddle horses. The cows were out on pasture, the broodmare bunch had been returned to their range, and the bulls were on their winter feed grounds.

Pat, Dwight, and I decided to do some hunting. I'd had Bud get me an elk license on one of his trips to town. I wasn't looking to get a trophy—a spike bull or dry cow is all I wanted. I was looking for meat rather than something to put on the wall. Pat and Dwight also had licenses, and Dwight was looking for a trophy bull. Pat was more interested in the meat.

"We didn't hold back a beef to kill for winter meat," said Pat.

"I noticed that," I said. "I was wondering what Bud had in mind."

"He might have been thinkin' he'd buy something at the 4-H sale," said Pat. "He's supported that quite a bit in the past. If we can get a couple of elk, we could probably save him some money, although he'd probably buy a hog or two and a steer at the sale just to help the kids out. He says it's also good for the ranch, supportin' the community an' the like."

"What, no lamb?"

"Nope," answered Pat. "His brother Rod will probably bring somethin' over in the sheep line, a lamb or ewe. He's generally done somethin' like that in the past."

We did the chores early the next day and went elk hunting. Dwight wanted to go horseback and we let him.

Pat and I opted to go in my truck and that's what we did. We put a saw and a block and tackle in the back of the truck and left. We drove for about an hour over the rough back roads, then selected a spot to park on a bluff overlooking a big open valley.

"We should see something here," said Pat.

"I know," I said, "I've seen elk here before. I would say our chances are pretty good."

"We can probably sit right here and get something."

"I think I'll get out an' get a better look in the bottom of that valley," I said. I got out and went over to the rim of the bluff. As soon as I got to the edge, I stopped and started backing up. I motioned for Pat to come toward me and pointed down toward the bottom of the valley. Quietly, Pat walked toward me.

"There's a big bull down there with about fifteen or twenty cows," I whispered. "They're on the bottom of this hill, on this side, that's why we couldn't see 'em from the truck. There should be some spike bulls off to the side, let's watch 'em awhile before we shoot. Make sure we got some spikes rather than dry cows."

"Sounds good to me," said Pat. "Too bad Dwight ain't here. That's a good bull."

"That's all right," I said. "I'd rather eat one like the young one comin' out of the trees across the valley. Lets see if another one follows him."

Shortly after the younger bull came out of the trees, another one followed.

"Which one do you want?"

"I don't care," I said. "Which one do you want?"

"I'll take the one farthest away," said Pat.

"Okay, tell me when you're ready."

"I'm ready now," said Pat, unlocking the safety on his rifle.

I brought my rifle to my shoulder. "Now," I said.

We both fired and both spikes went down. The spike that was farthest away tried to get up and run off, but without success. The herd of cows and big bull, hearing the shots, ran toward the trees and disappeared from sight.

"I'll go down an' finish him off," said Pat. "You bring the truck as best as you can."

"See you at the bottom," I said, as I started to the truck. "It'll take me awhile to get there." Shortly, I heard another shot and figured Pat had finished off the spike.

By the time I got to the bottom with the truck, Pat had started on his elk. I left the truck with Pat and went to the elk I'd shot and cut his throat to let him bleed out. Both spikes were in good shape and I thought they'd be some good eating.

Pat called me over. "Give me a hand with this an' we'll be done here." Pat had split the hide down the middle of the elk from his brisket to his hindquarters. He took the saw and sawed the brisket bone.

I helped Pat with rigging the block and tackle and we hoisted the spike up along the side of the truck, then we gutted the elk.

"If I'd have thought," said Pat, "we'd have hoisted the end gate an' split him right down the middle there. Now we'll have to turn him an' try to saw down his backbone. Hold him steady Honey, I'll start. We'll do yours a different way, it'll be easier."

We got the elk sawed in half then quartered him. We left what we didn't want, like the legs from the knees down and the head. "We should have brought some meat sacks, the back of your truck is filthy." said Pat. "Or you should clean out the back of your truck more often!"

"It's all right," I said. "We'll leave the hide on an' that'll keep this stuff off him. This still beats ridin' all day, then havin' to pack one out horseback."

"Yep," said Pat. "Now let's get yours."

I drove the truck to where my elk had fallen. We made the cleaning process considerably easier than it was with Pat's elk with the truck handy. It wasn't long before we had my elk cleaned and quartered and laying in the back if the truck.

"Head out this way," said Pat. "There's an old road down there an' even though it'll take us longer to get back, it'll be easier than tryin' to go up that hill. How'd you get down it?"

"Very carefully," I answered, "very carefully."

Pat laughed. "I'll bet it was fun! I wonder how Dwight's doin'. I haven't heard any shots from the direction he said he was goin'."

Suddenly, I stopped the truck. "I think we'd better tag these elk before we go much farther. I see some dust off in the distance an' don't know who it is."

"You're right," said Pat. "I'd plumb forgot about taggin' 'em. I don't think it would look good if our boss's brother arrested us for poachin'."

Pat laughed and so did I. But I remembered when Bud's brother Rod shot a deer out of season and Fred showed up that night and ate with us. I was going to tell Pat about the incident, but decided not to. The fewer people that knew about it, the better off we were.

We got to the ranch and hung the elk quarters in the barn. We finished skinning them and put them in some meat sacks. They'd be cool enough in the barn. As we were finishing up, Dwight came riding in.

I asked, "How's the huntin'?"

"Pretty tough hunting today, I didn't see anything."

"We got ours," said Pat, "just a couple of spikes. But there was a monster bull with them. He must have been the grand-daddy of 'em all. I don't think I've ever seen a bull so big."

Pat was laying it on a little thick, having some fun with Dwight. And Dwight was drinking it all in! Dwight's mouth dropped open a little more with each comment Pat made.

"It's a good thing you weren't with us," continued Pat. "If you'd have shot him, we'd still be out there tryin' to get him cleaned an' loaded in the truck!"

"Where was this at? I'd like to go out there tomorrow and see if I can get him."

"We don't want you to get him," said Pat. "It would take a front-end loader to get him in the truck if you did get him! That's a lot of work."

I got a little tired of this line of bull, but Dwight was taking it all in. I took the hearts and livers of the elk to the cook.

"Do you want these tonight? It ain't too late to fix them up," said the cook.

"Whatever you want," I said.

"This visceral stuff is generally better the day it's shot. I'll fix it up for tonight."

Sally came in. "What's up?"

"We're having heart and liver from your husband," said the cook.

"From my husband! What will he do without them?"

"I thought you thought I didn't have a heart," I said.

"I can see you have one. There's even two on the table. Did you get both of them?"

"No," I said. "Pat got one and I got one. Poor Dwight, he hunted all day an' didn't even see anythin'."

"He'll have other chances. He might learn to go where people who know the country go."

"He was in a good area, there just weren't any elk there today."

At supper that night, Bud was very appreciative of the wild game meat. "I forgot to hold back a beef when we sold our cattle. I'll probably go to the 4-H sale and get something just to help out some of the kids."

"Better get three hogs this year," said the cook. "We ran short of pork last year."

We weren't busy the next few days and Dwight continued to hunt, but without success. He wanted Pat and I to take him out to where we'd got our spikes, but we declined.

"Those elk are long gone," said Pat. "Give 'em a few days an' they'll probably return. Be patient, that's the secret. But if we're goin' out there, we're takin' the truck. We'd need too many horses to bring the bull home if you do get him!"

We rode our country on a regular basis and Dwight continued to carry a rifle with him as we rode. He was still hoping for that trophy bull, although Pat had laid it on so thick, I was sure Dwight was catching on.

On one occasion, we met some hunters that were hunting on our land, even though it was posted. Bud had sold some hunting permits at the ranch, but these people hadn't bought one.

"Do you know you're huntin' on posted ground?" I was trying to be polite with these people.

"No," they answered.

"There's a sign posted right by the gate where you entered our property. It says 'Hunting by Permission Only.' I nailed it there myself. If you want to hunt here, you'll need to buy a permit. They cost twenty-five dollars an' they're good for the huntin' season. If you don't want to buy a permit, you'll have to leave. It's as simple as that."

"I think twenty-five dollars is kind of expensive," said the hunter. "I don't think I want to pay it."

"Go ahead an' pay it," said another hunter, "we've been camped here three days already."

"I think it's too expensive and I won't pay it. What's he going to do, call a cop? Out here? Don't be silly."

"If you don't want to pay it and don't want to leave, we'll call the game warden an' let him conclude the deal."

"Hah! You just go ahead," said the hunter. The hunter seemed to be very arrogant.

He looked surprised when I took out the two-way radio and called the ranch.

"Hello, Bud? Better call Fred. We've got some hunters out here that have been camped out here three days an' don't want to buy a permit an' don't want to leave. Their license number is ..." I read the number off of their truck and gave Bud the make and color.

"I'll call Fred right now," said Bud. "Do you know where they're camped?"

"We'll find out and report it to you."

"I don't know where Fred is right now, but I'll call him and he'll be there as soon as he can. You know, he kinda likes these deals."

"I think he's running a bluff," said the one hunter.

I told Bud where we were and we left to look for the hunter's camp. We found out where they were camped and I called Bud and gave him the information.

"Fred's on the way right now," said Bud. "You guys stick close just in case he needs some help. He's not as young as he used to be. Keep your eyes on the intruders."

"They haven't made any move to break camp," I said. "We'll head back to the place where we met them an' wait for Fred there."

Soon we saw the game warden's truck headed our way. Fred was not alone; he had a helper, a big, strapping kind of guy. Fred's helper looked like a football player.

I met Fred when he got out of the truck. He came up and shook hands with Pat and myself. "This is Agent Wilkerson, my assistant. This is Honey and Pat."

We shook hands with Agent Wilkerson as he said, "Donald, just call me Don."

"Where's our culprits? They're not here," said Fred.

"There out huntin'," I said. "Their camp is over there, just behind that rise. We'll ride over to it with you."

"They haven't been in camp since we first saw them," said Pat. "They'll be around somewhere."

We took the game wardens to the hunters' camp. We could see the dust from their truck rising as they returned to their camp.

"Looks like that's them coming now. Honey, you and Pat stick around and make sure that it's the right guys."

Pat and I both said, "Yes."

The truck approached and I recognized it as the offending hunters.

Fred was very professional in his approach to the hunters. He asked, "Do you know you're trespassing?"

"No sir," came the reply from the arrogant hunter. He didn't seem quite as arrogant as he was earlier.

"Well, you are," said Fred. "Has this young man given you the option of hunting here or leaving?"

"Yes," said the hunter, "but I thought it was too high. Twenty-five bucks!"

"I understand you've been here three days. Is that correct?"

"Yes sir," was the reply.

"How was the hunting?"

"I did get a small deer. We're just going to use him for camp meat."

Don asked, "Did you tag him?"

"Not yet," the hunter answered.

"Technically, not tagging the animal at the spot of the kill is breaking the law. Where's the carcass?"

"Hanging in that tree," answered the hunter. Don went over and checked the carcass.

"The deer is not tagged and you're trespassing. You've broken the law. I'm going to cite you." He took out his book and started to write a ticket.

"You can pay the fine and forfeit your hunting privileges for three years or show up in court with a lawyer and defend yourselves. I'm writing you both up on charges of failure to properly tag your animal and trespassing. The Wilson ranch will make a decision as to whether or not to press charges in a civil matter. You need to show me your hunting licenses and drivers' licenses."

The hunters got out their licenses and Agent Wilkerson wrote the tickets. While he was doing that, Pat and Fred were having a discussion.

"Don is fairly new to the warden's office," said Fred. "How do you think he handled the situation?"

"I thought he was very professional," said Pat.

"So did I," said Fred. "You know he's a former police officer."

"I didn't know that," said Pat, half-way laughing. "I thought you had taught him all that professional stuff."

"Careful," said Fred, "or I'll write you up for hunting without a gun!"

They both laughed heartily and it was apparent they had known each other for a long time.

"I think it might be a good idea if you game wardens stuck around until these guys broke camp and left. You might want to follow them off the property," I said.

"That was my intention, Honey," said Fred.

One of the hunters asked, "What's this honey stuff?"

"That's his name," said Fred. "He's famous around here. He was instrumental in catching some would-be horse thieves last summer. He made the front page in our local paper after the trial and was the star witness for the prosecution."

The hunter didn't seem impressed.

Pat and I stayed around and visited with Fred and Don while the hunters hastily broke camp. Don was a nice feller, seemingly easy to get along with. Before they left, following the hunters, I invited him to the Wilson ranch.

"Fred," I said, "you know you're always welcome."

Pat and I got on our horses as they all drove away.

"I don't guess they'll be back," said Pat.

"Not for a while," I said.

Bud met us as we rode into the barn. "What was the outcome?"

"Fred's partner wrote them out tickets, an' Fred an' his partner followed 'em off the property. Don't know what they'll do; pay 'em or go to court," I said.

"I guess we'll find out. What's this about Fred's partner? I hadn't heard anything."

"Yeah," said Pat. "He's got a partner, an ex cop. But he's a real nice guy. Honey here even invited him out to the ranch."

"Yep," I said. "I think it's a good idea to stay on the right side of the law. By the way Bud, do you think we've been unduly involved with the law this year? We've had the sheriff out here for the horse stealers this year, an' the game warden out here for the trespassers this year, an' the sheriff an' the game warden out here last season for the drunken hunter. To me, it seems a little out of the ordinary to be involved with the law so much."

"It's a little unusual," said Bud, "but if that's what it takes, we'll do it. The law is here to protect the public and punish the lawbreakers. As long as we're not lawbreakers, we're doing our part."

Pat laughed as he put his saddle away. Bud gave him a funny look, but didn't say anything.

Noticing this, I said, "I've got the feelin', for some reason or another, that this place ain't always been the little piece of heaven that you want to make it out to be."

"Well," said Bud, "perhaps it hasn't been. Someday I'll tell you about it."

I'd suspected that the ranch might have had a past that was a little shady, and now, or whenever Bud got around to it, I was going to find out something about it. I knew it wouldn't do any good to press him about it; he'd tell me in his own time, when he was ready.

"I've sold about twenty hunting permits this year and the cook has sold a few. It's been almost as profitable as taking hunters out and a lot easier. But I'll be glad when hunting season is over. For some reason or another, hunters always seem to cause more trouble than your everyday tourists."

"Of course," said Pat. "Give a city slicker a loaded gun an' turn him loose in the open an' he becomes a different person. Primordial instinct, is that what they call it? I'm not sure, but I'll be just as happy as you are when the season's over. But their money is just as good as anybody else's. Sometimes I wonder if it's really worth it."

"Me too," said Bud.

I agreed.

Into the Winter

The hunting season didn't pass without incident. One morning I woke up to the faint smell of smoke in the air. Bud was already up, making the golf cart ready to check out the smoky smell.

"Come with me," I said. "We'll take the truck an' find out what this is all about. Some of the hunters might have let their fire get away from them." I brought my truck around for Bud to get into and we started out to look for the fire.

We found it, about three miles from the lodge. I felt fortunate that what little wind there was, was blowing the fire away from the lodge and corrals. Bud called the cook back at the lodge.

"Better call the BLM and ask their help in putting this thing out," he told the cook. "We don't have the equipment to do it here. I'm guessing it's covered about seven or eight acres so far. Honey and I are about three, maybe four miles from the lodge. We'll stay here and wait for the BLM if they're coming. Call me back and let me know what they're doing."

"I'll call them as soon as I can," said the cook. "Pat and Dwight and Sally are headed your direction. They've got the pickup and the two-ton truck with a couple of tow chains and a bunch of old tires. I think they want to make a fire line by dragging the tires between the trucks."

"It might work," said Bud. "At least it's something. But you get the BLM out here as soon as you can!"

There wasn't much we could do. I did have a shovel in the back of my truck. I grabbed it and started using it to smother little hot spots that were developing. It wasn't much, but it was all I could do. Pat and Dwight showed up and rigged the tires between the trucks to make a drag. I doubted that it would work, but it was worth a try.

Sally had come out with Pat. She grabbed a shovel and started helping me take care of the hot spots. Bud sat in my truck watching helplessly.

Dwight and Pat made a trip around the leading edge of the fire dragging the tires between them. They turned around and started back. I thought they were doing some good, but I couldn't tell how much. I thought if they slowed down, they might do more good. I also thought if Sally and I followed them, we could put out the hot spots with the shovels. With some luck, we might get this thing contained.

When Pat and Dwight got to me, Pat stopped and asked, "Are we doin' any good, Honey?"

"I think so," I said. "You might want to go a little slower, the tires are bouncing up and down an' not draggin' the whole area. Sally an' me can come along an' hit the hot spots."

"We'll give it a try," said Pat, as he motioned to Dwight to start again. They started out slower and Sally and I followed, putting out the hot spots.

Soon I noticed a vehicle approaching from the direction in which the fire had started. "The BLM," I thought. "We'll soon have this under control!"

But it wasn't the BLM. It was hunters. They had seen the smoke and came to investigate. They stopped at my truck where Bud was watching and he sent them over to where Sally and I were working.

"Can we help?"

"Sure," I said. "If you got some shovels, get 'em an' help put out these little hot spots." There were three hunters, two men and a teenage boy. They had one shovel and one of the men grabbed it and started after the hot spots.

"Let me spell you," said the other man as he took my shovel. The boy went and took Sally's shovel.

"I'll go back to the ranch an' get some more shovels," I said.

"I'll go with you," said Sally.

I went back to my truck and drove to the barn. On the way, Sally and Bud discussed the situation. Bud was almost cussing the hunters.

"You can wait here until we get this thing handled," I told Bud when we got to the barn. I threw a couple of shovels in the back of the truck.

"No," he said. "I need to be out there." There wasn't much he could do, but he wanted to be out there.

We started back toward the fire. On the way, we noticed more vehicles approaching the fire zone.

"I hope that's the BLM," I said.

"It is," said Bud. "And it looks like they've got a dozer on that trailer. With that dozer, we'll have this licked in no time!"

We pulled up to where the BLM trucks had stopped. They were unloading the dozer off the trailer. The fellow in charge of the BLM crew came over and shook hands with Bud. They already knew each other.

"Pat and Dwight are trying to make a fire break out there," said Bud, pointing toward where the two trucks were moving.

"We'll take the dozer and give them a hand," said the BLM crew chief. "We've got some water trucks and can spray these hot spots. But keep your people working on them. I'll have a few fellers help them. We'll have this little thing licked pretty quick. Good thing you called us early."

I got a shovel and went back to putting out the hot spots. After the dozer went by, the water trucks came by and sprayed water on the fire break.

"Keep an eye outside the fire break," said the driver. "Look for sparks the wind may have blown over there."

Those of us using shovels changed our tactics and looked outside the fire break for sparks.

Dwight and Pat got their trucks and tires out of the way when they saw the dozer coming. But they continued dragging the tires, outside the fire line. They stopped when they got to me.

"We'll have this thing licked before long," said Pat. "Good thing the BLM showed up. This could have gotten out of hand pretty fast."

"We might have been pretty lucky today," I said. "We need to find out where an' how this thing got started. After we're sure this is under control, we'll talk to those hunters that showed up an' see if we can find out about this. The permits Bud sold all the hunters might give us some help. I think we can search around with the help of the BLM crew chief an' find where this started."

The water trucks made another pass then went to the creek, about a mile away, to refill the tanks.

I told Sally, "Keep a close eye on this until the water trucks get back. We need to keep on top of this!"

The water trucks arrived and started to spray the area again. Soon we had the fire out.

Bud and the BLM crew chief were talking to the hunters that had come to help. I asked Bud, "What's those hunters' story?"

"They saw the smoke and came to see what was happening," said Bud. "They appear to have just been trying to help. I don't think they had anything to do with the fire getting started."

"I think we ought to get the crew chief and see if we can find out where this thing started," I said. "We can go in my truck."

The BLM crew chief said, "Why don't you follow me? I'll take my truck."

"Whatever you say," I said.

We drove back in the direction the fire had come from, hoping to find where and how it had started. Occasionally, the crew chief would stop and put out a hot spot.

"Once those cow chips start smoldering they can smolder for days, then if a little wind comes up they can start another fire," he explained. "You guys keep your eyes open for them and when you see them, stop and put them out. Use your shovel or boot or whatever."

We followed the crew chief. Eventually he stopped. "You guys stay in your truck," he said. "I want to look for tracks."

I stayed in the truck. Bud didn't have a choice. Eventually, the crew chief motioned me over.

"It looks to me like the fire started here, probably by some hunter that built himself a warming fire and didn't get it out all the way. That's my guess." I went back and reported the crew chief's conclusions to Bud.

"We'll probably never be able to find out who started it and prove it. I'm thinking the hunters are more trouble than they're worth!" said Bud.

"I think you're right," I said.

We went back to where Pat and everyone else were waiting. The BLM crew was still looking for hot spots.

"I think this is probably under control now," said Pat. "We need to go back an' do our chores."

"You're right," said Bud. "Honey, take me over to the BLM crew chief, I want to thank him."

"I'm going home with you," said Sally.

Pat and Dwight had already unhooked the tires and loaded them and the chains in the back of the trucks, then they left. Bud, Sally, and I went to the crew chief. Bud thanked him and invited him to the ranch any time, then we went back to the lodge.

On the way, Bud said, "Sometimes I think this place is driving me crazy!"

"Don't let it get to you," said Sally. "You always told me to make the best of whatever happens."

"You're right, daughter, you're right! We can overcome all these little setbacks, although it might take a little time. We just need to stay positive!"

"Interesting words from a person whose world was slowly closing in on him," I thought.

Other Books by Stu Campbell

Horsing Around a Lot

Horsing Around the Dudes

Humor Around Horses

You Can't Be Serious!

Comedy Around the Corral

More Humor Around Horses

A Young Cowboy's Adventure

Honey

Surprise!